# TOUCHED BY THE MAGIC

## BOOK TWO

## LOUISE RIVEIRO-MITCHELL

Cover design by Outlaws Publishing LLC
Published by Outlaws Publishing LLC
June 2024
10987654321

It is said there is a magic in that territory they call Montana. Those who have been touched by it know it's true. Come and find that magic and be touched by it too.

**Dedication:**

I dedicate this book to my father, Antonio Riveiro, who at an early age instilled the love of westerns and cowboys in my heart and soul and my Tio Paco Francisco Lago who taught me to love history that gave me the foundation for my writing. I hope I please them with my words and honor their memory.

## Chapter 1

Sleep had not come easy for Cully, nor had the assignment he was asked to undertake. He knew there were at least four – five others like himself that could take this assignment with no problem and who were still in the army. But when Cully told this to the secretary, the gentleman told him he was chosen by the president himself and he would not accept no for an answer. Cully knew what they were suggesting would shred any thoughts of peace between the Indians and the whites.

It had been a long argument with the Indians to remove the prospectors from the hills. Land that was given to the Indians and now taken away. Taken from them with new prospectors arriving each day looking for that strike to make them wealthy. And now they want to bring more men into the territory, not to strip the land of the gold, but to build miles and miles of track so the trains can travel through the Indian land, without their permission. Soon these iron horses as the Indians called them would take settlers to this land, soon these settlers would stay and build on land that was not theirs and the Indians would be called savages when they tried to fight for their land.

True, all the reasons for the railroad going through the territory looked and sounded good back in Washington. Of course back there where nary an Indian could be found and streets were paved, and corners where they had street lamps that lit up the road; you could see almost as good as daylight. Why some of those fine gentlemen in the congress and senate haven't been back in their state in years, but they knew what those folk who voted them into their office needed and how a railroad was gonna help 'em. Yep, seems like them men really knew what was best for the people. But then again that's what they been telling them all these years. Now there be those who will tell ya that the railroad is progress, that it will unite the east and west for the first time.

Cully knows what the railroad will do to those fine folk back east, it will make them rich, but what will it do to the Indian? That seems to be the question no one wants to think about. Granted, there are railroads that travel to certain parts of the country, but this whole idea of saving time by cutting across the mountains just doesn't seem to work out. There are a number of if's that could happen. If the snow comes early and the tracks are covered, an avalanche, a number of other problems were getting to those stranded would be impossible, what then?

He gets up from his bed and walks over to the window and looks out at the moonlight shining outside. His thoughts drift off to Liss and wondered if she too was up looking out her window. He thought about if she would think he just decided to not go back. Oh he could never do that, but how would she know? She only knew him for those few days. Oh how he wished he had decided to stay back there with her instead of riding on to the fort. He closed his eyes and for a moment; her face came to mind. There was no mistaking it, she was a beautiful gal and she didn't even know it. He realized he had to give his answer in a few hours to the captain and as much as he'd rather go back to the Circle C, he didn't feel he could get out of this easy, especially with the president not taking no for an answer. He looked up at the moon and smiled, "you will make sure she'll understand, right?"

Slowing, he made his way back to the cot and fell asleep only to be jerked back awake by the sound of the dang bugle. He stumbled to the door when he heard the light rap on the door. He opened the door to find Corporal Reynolds smiling there with his breakfast tray in his hands, "morning sir, I took the liberty of bringing you your breakfast."

"Well that's very considerate of you Corporal." He watched the young lad as he placed the tray on the desk. Corporal Reynolds looked up at him and smiled, "Sir?"

"Have you eaten your breakfast yet?"

"No Sir, I was …"

Cully smiles at him," well then I insist you sit right down and have this delicious breakfast."

"Oh, but Sir I…"

"Now Corporal that's a direct order, I insist you eat now."

The young man looks at him, "now I insist Corporal."

With that Cully opens the door to leave when he turns and looks at the boy." By the way Corporal, what is your name?"

The boy smiles at him, "Reynolds Sir, Martin Reynolds."

"Well Marty, you sit there and finish your breakfast, we have a full day ahead."

The lad smiles at Cully who in turn leaves and heads toward the captain's office.

With a gentle rap he enters the captain's office.

The captain looks up from his desk, "good morning, Cully have you eaten your breakfast already?"

Cully looks at him, "well tell you the truth, I'm not much of a breakfast person. I'm still a bit concerned on this assignment. I mean I do know for a fact, Major Kincaid is more capable for this, why me?"

Doug looks at him, there was no use in lying to him. He looks up from his breakfast. "Cully, you are the one who can possibly pull this off. After all, your grandmother, Evening Star, was the daughter of Black Hawk. Seems tribes are. well; they set kindly on one of their own.

Cully looks at him, "you mean them yahoos in Washington think who my grandma was will give them a free pass into Indian territory?"

Doug knew Cully would not take this news well. "Cully, it's not my doing."

Cully looks at him, "maybe so, but you could have suggested someone else. hell Doug, I spent four years in a war I didn't want no part of. Four years of seeing folks I grew up with fighting each other."

The captain looked at him, "look, your men will be ready to set out for the mountain pass. If you're lucky you can get there and be back in two days with the prospectors. Remember no one is to be left there."

Cully looks at him, "now who would want to stay there?" After he said it, he thought on it, there was talk of that yellow stuff that turns a man's head to dreams of a better life that is always in their dreams and hiding from reality. He looks at Doug, "yea, I'll make sure they all come back."

Doug gets up from his desk and they walk out of the office where the troops are assembled and ready to ride. Cully mounts his horse then looks at Doug, "I'll see you back here in four days, Captain."

Doug looks at him, "I'll be expecting you."

Cully nods and heads toward the gates of the fort and leads the troops out.

Back at the Circle C, the sun is up and it's a new day at the ranch. Liss is getting dressed and about to head down for breakfast. For a moment, she stops and looks toward the window. *It's been three days since Cully left for Fort Bennett. He had promised he'd return. Did he really mean it or was it just a line for him to exit gracefully? Did he plan on leaving and never to return? Still she couldn't help but wonder. He did sound earnest.* True he was only at the ranch a mere three days, but they were three days that left an impression on Liss' heart. The more she thought about him the more she realized she really knew nothing about this man, but that he had come into her life and then he was gone. She kept asking herself what was this hold he had on her yet was it a hold on her yet the answer was, she didn't know.

Her thoughts were brought back to the present when she heard her mother's voice calling to her from the bottom of the stairs, "Melissa, breakfast is ready, come on down." She opens the door and heads down the stairs. Seeing that her mother was in the kitchen this would be the perfect time for her to head out the door and to the barn. As she reaches the door her father walks in and startles her, "Papa!"

"Good morning Kitten, goin' somewhere?"

"No, I was… Well I was looking for you Papa."

He put his arm around her shoulder knowing that was not the real reason, but they walked toward the dining room, "well you found me, so let's go and have some breakfast." They walked in to see Jason sitting at the table and Liz walking into the room with a fresh pot of coffee.

Jason smiles at Eli and then Liss. "Good morning Liss."

She smiles at him.

Jason was the big brother she wished she had, always there for her, always watching her. Oh there was a time a few years back she even had an infatuation for him. She had to admit he was handsome. He was that knight in shunning armor who would ride up and take her away to a land where they would spend their lives together. But that was a lifetime ago or so it seemed.

Jason turned his attention to Eli, "Sir, I noticed some fence in the south range was down, I figured I'd take a few men and have it tended to today, if it's alright with you.'"

Eli looks up at him as he takes a sip of his coffee, "fine, you can start on that right after breakfast."

"Yes sir."

They continue eating breakfast as Eli looks over to Liss and smiles at her. Suddenly, Liss gets up and starts to leave when Liz looks at her, "and where do you think you're going?"

"Oh I thought I'd go and saddle up and help with the…." She looks at her mother and has a feeling she's not going anywhere."

"You are staying here and help me get this house ready for the welcome home party tonight.'"

"But Mama…"

"I will not hear any excuse Melissa, you are old enough now to take on some of responsibilities of this ranch that is a women's duty. And it's time you realize that one of the responsibilities of running a ranch from a woman's point of view is preparing for events."

"But Mama…."

"I'll not hear another word Melissa, you are to stay here today and help me with the preparations." With that she hands her breakfast plate to Liss and points to the kitchen door.

It was a long ride to the mountain camp and there was no way these soldier boys were not being watched every step of the way. Seems the Indians didn't really give permission for those men to prospect on their land matter of fact they hadn't given anyone to even set afoot in those hills. Seems the solider boys done took it on themselves to let a group of men head on into the hills and when one found that shiny gold rocks, more and a more kept on a comin'.

And now what the Indians feared would happen. Now the soldiers were coming and maybe more men to take those gold rocks out of the hills. Cully kept feeling that as they got closer to the mountain they were being watched and it wasn't an easy feeling he had. By evening, they would make camp right at the beginning of the mountain pass, by tomorrow they would reach the mining camp. If all went well, they would be headin' for the fort in two days. That's if all went well.

Cully looked over his shoulder, still he wished he didn't feel something still wasn't right. It was just before sun-down, Cully and the men set up camp for the night. The meal was simple, beans, biscuits and coffee, but the men weren't 'spectin' a gourmet meal, not out here anyway.

Corporal Reynolds came to sit beside Cully. He was a nice enough kid, a little green behind the ears, but he did have grit and he did want to learn. In a few years, the good Lord willing, he may rise up in the ranks. He reminded Cully of another young man back home. Same sandy blond hair, blue eyes and a smile that he was a fine boy. So excited he was to go off and join the army, so excited to prove he was a man. It was on the hot July day in a place called Gettysburg that young boy and so many others faced their fate and became part of history.

A while later, unable to sleep, Cully gets up and walks over to the campfire. He still had a feeling that somewhere sometime they were gonna run into some

Indians. He sat down looking into the flames; how he wished he was anywhere but there. And then his mind went back to Liss Crawford. He just couldn't for the life of him figure why no one ever noticed the gal. Okay he did think she was a boy at first but…. *Well there was somthin' 'bout those eyes of hers. Well, she's probably forgotten about him anyway after all it was only a brief meeting and one can't form any type of relationship in just three days*. He thought about that again, just three days and he can't seem to get her out of his mind. But it would have to wait for another time.

It seemed like only minutes ago that Cully fell asleep, but it was time to move out. It was Corporal Reynolds who was Cully's shadow. Wherever he was, the young boy was not far behind.

"Morning Sir."

Cully looked up at him and smiled, "good morning Martin. Ready to move out?"

"Yes Sir."

Cully smiled, "well let's get this company saddled up."

Martin smiled and headed off to the remuda where the horses were.

It wasn't long before Cully was ready to get his troops together and start for the mountains. With a little bit of luck they could be out of those mountains before the Sioux even knew they was there. As the sun was rising in the sky, Cully kept looking at the ridge to the side of them. If there was anywhere for the attack to come from it would be from there.

Suddenly, the sound of a rifle is heard and directly ahead is a group of miners armed and not too happy to see the soldiers. "That's just about fer enough Soldier Boy."

Cully looks at the miner, "we wish no harm on you or the other miners. I have been sent here from the president to escort you out of these mountains and back to Fort Bennett."

The miner looks Cully and the men, then back to Cully. "Well you can just gti back to the fort and tell your president, we's not leaving our claims so's you fine gentlemen can steal our claims."

Cully looks at him, "You don't understand you all are breaking the treaty by digging on land that was given to the Sioux."

The miner took a step closer to Cully, still with the riffle in his hand, "you is the one who don't understand Solider Boy, we are owners of this here piece of rock and we have the papers to prove it."

Cully could see this was not going to be easy. Slowly he dismounts, "Sir, I am Michael Patrick Culhane and I have been sent here by the president of...."

He miner stopped him '' you mean to tell me you ain't no solider boy?"

"No sir, I'm not."

A smile came to the man's face, "well what the hell is you doing with all those Yankee blue bellies?"

Trying to hide his smile Cully looks back at the man, "and to who do I have the pleasure of speaking with?"

The man looked at him and lowered the rifle, "Captain Nathaniel Montgomery Carter of the Confederate Army of the state of Tennessee Sir." With that he gives a salute to which Cully salutes him back.

"Well Captain Carter, you can understand orders and when they are given, they should be carried out.'"

"I do see your point there, but being that we was given this here land...."

Cully stops him… "Captain Carter, who gave you this land and when?"

"Well near as I kin figure, it was after the war and these fellas came into town, ya know them fancy dressed eastern dudes. Well they came to town with promises of gold for all. They said all we had to do was come out here to Montana and set up our claims and half of everything we prospect would be ours."

Cully looked on as the men behind him nodded in agreement, he then turns his attention to the man in front of him, "so these fellas come into your town telling you that they would give you half of everything you found?"

The old man nods, "yes sir, them were his exact words." He looks at Cully, "you meaning to say we ain't a gonna git what we's been promised?"

"Well I can't say anything for sure Mr. Carter, but if you and your men come back to the fort with us, I guarantee to all of you, I will find out where your money is and who has it."

The old ma smiles at Cully, "you know Soldier Boy, you being alright for a Yankee."

Cully smiled back at him; he didn't have the heart to tell him he was on the same side as he was in the war. Didn't make much difference anymore. It was time to heal the wounds and we had to once again be united.

It was early afternoon when the miners had their belongings packed on the wagons and were ready to head with the army back to Fort Bennett.

As the caravan moved closer to the pass, Cully got that feeling again. He hadn't seen any reason to worry, but that feeling was still there. It was the young corporal who first noticed them on the ridge. "Captain Cully!"

Cully looks at the direction the young boy was pointing to, "everyone take cover behind the rocks!"

A band of Sioux headed down the mountain only to meet the rifles of the boys from Fort Bennett.

Cully looked at Carter, "now you see why I was telling you why you needed ta get out of the mountain."

The older men nods and continues shooting.

The skirmish only lasted till the Indians figured they made their point. They slowly made their way back behind the mountain as Cully and his men assessed their casualties and what was lost. Cully knew they best be mounting up and heading for the fort. He looked around at the group of men. "It's time we best getting down the pass and as far away from here as fast as we can."

Back at the fort, Doug Stiles stands by the sentry post looking out for any sign of Cully and the men returning. He'd been up there for quite a spell when Dr. Witherspoon decided to go look for him, maybe he needed some company or just someone to watch the trail with him.

The old doc struck a match to light his pipe as he looks over to Doug, "you look worried Doug? Maybe your friend wasn't the right choice after all?"

He looks at the doctor, "Doc, I've known Cully since we were both kids. Sure, we came from different worlds and he wasn't given all the breaks in life I was, but I'm willing to put my army career on the line for him. Why, the ain't no other person I'd want on my side in a fight but him."

The doctor looks at him seriously, "you care a great deal about him don't ya? Let me guess, he saved your life."

Doug looked at him, "he saved the entire regiment's lives. You see Cully's grandmother was Evening Star, daughter of Black Hawk."

The doctor looked at him. "The Sioux Chief Black Hawk?"

Doug nodded, the very same one."

The doctor let out a long sigh. "Black Hawk was one of the Chiefs at Big Horn. Why…"

Doug didn't let him go on. "Well it seems Cully's grandpa was a trapper who made a living on the furs and well, he had a peaceful relationship with the Indians.

It was about the fourth year he found himself stuck up in the mountains and would likely die if it hadn't been for Black Hawk. He and his braves were out on a hunting trip for the village. They ran into old Jebez Culhane, seems he got stuck up in the hills and well; was almost gone when they found him. Black Hawk had heard of the white trapper who trapped furs and left everything else for the Indians. He saw no reason not to help the man. With the help of his braves they took grandpa back to the village."

The doctor looks at him. "And?"

Doug smiles him, "and then his grandpa married the chief's daughter, a pretty young girl named Evening Star. Well, they had three sons and grandpa had a trading post, so his wife was never far from her folks. Years passed by and old Jeb made the boys promise him on his death bed they would get their ma back to her folks.

It was the two older boys, James and John, that left with Evening Star to the high country and her people. Seems they never made it. With the recent Indian raids and how folks were a bit skittish at anyone that even looked Indian… well. seems these two fellas were hid up in the rocks they had been up there three days after being chased by Indians and they were too afraid to move from that spot. They heard the sound of horses and figured it was the Indians heading back for the chance to jump them."

Doc Witherspoon looks at him, "don't tell me."

"You got it. These three bumbling idiots attacked the two boys and their mother, killing all three. They then took off to town to tell the folks that the Indians were raiding farms in the area."

"And?"

Doug looked at him, "it was Cully's father who brought the bodies back and buried them near his pa. Three days later, he left the only home he ever knew and headed west. I believe he was only sixteen years old then. Got himself on a wagon train as a scout; few years later, I met up with him. I tell you one thing he may complain about this assignment, but he is the only person who could do it."

## Chapter 2

Suddenly, the sounds of horses from the distance could be heard and Doug spotted Cully ahead of the troops. A smile came to his face as he sees that he had done it. It got the miners out and back here to the fort.

"Cully!" He raced down to the gate and greeted the troops as they rode in.

Cully gets off his horse and starts to salute Doug, Michael Culhane Sir; mission has been executed and completed."

Cully was about to salute him when Doug grabs his hand and gives him a hug, "You crazy fool, you did it you got them out!"

He looked at his friend, "don't tell me you were worried about me?"

Doug smiled, "well course not, but I did worry about the horses, it's hard to get good horses out here."

They both start to laugh.

Cully turned to Carter standing beside him. then back to Doug, "Captain Stiles, may I present to you, Captain Nathaniel Montgomery Carter retired from the Confederate Army of America."

Doug stood at attention and saluted the man, Captain, welcome to Fort Bennett, I hope your stay will be a pleasant one."

The older man salutes him back and nods, "on behalf of my men here and myself we thank you. If'in you just tell us where we can bunk down till all this gets settled, I'd be muchly obliged."

Doug looks at Cully. "Well you see Doug, Captain Carter and his men… Maybe it would be better if we talked in your office. Captain, would you mind joining us?"

The man shook his head and all four men walked toward the office. After Doug heard the story and though he did feel badly for Nathaniel and his men, his hands were tied, but he promised to send a report to Washington and have these men brought up on charges. But it was in the meantime when all these men had worked so hard and had nothing to send to their families back home. Families who were patiently waiting for word that they could come out here and be with their husbands.

"Doug, there has to be something we could do for these men."

"I'd like to help Cully, but..."

"Don't give me that I'd like to help Doug, these men..."

Doug looked at him, "like I said, I will send a wire to Washington, I'll even keep the miners here until we get an answer ..."

Cully pulls Doug aside and away from the others, "look I know there's only so much you can do, but these folks have lost everything since the war ended. They are proud men Doug, when they were offered a job that would not only make them feel useful again it was a way to settle in new territory and bring their families and once again feel part of this country of ours. Didn't your Mr. Lincoln say it's time to bind up those wounds and make us the great nation we are? All I can say is if'in someone offered me everything I could take out of the earth I'd do the same as these men."

The captain looks at his friend. He knows how passionate Cully could get for a cause he believed in, but he never had that look in his eyes. There was something in that spark in his eyes that his old friend has found someone, someone who could make this wandering drifter want to dream of putting down roots and settling down. He smiles at Cully, "who is she?"

"She?"

"The gal who's got you dreaming of shoes and rice. Come on."

Cully walks back over to the miners, "I'll have Corporal Reynolds take you all over to the telegraph office here and you can all send wires to your families, let them know you're alright and will wire them soon when you know more."

Carter looks at Cully, "you meaning we can go back to the hills young fella?"

Cully pats the man's shoulder, "I'm gonna see what can be done for you Mr. Carter."

The old man held out his hand, "thank ya Son. Thank ya kindly."

Cully smiles, then looks at the corporal, "Martin, I want you to help these gentlemen get settled here and help them with anything they need."

The young man nods and begins leading the men out of the captain's office.

Once gone Doug looks at Cully, "I'm waiting?"

Cully smiles and heads for the door, "I'll be back in a bit Doug, I just remembered something."

He heads out the door hearing Doug calling out his name. Oh he knew sooner or later he would have to tell Doug about Liss, but for now, he'd rather keep the information for later than sooner. Oh he wasn't jealous or anything like that, it's just that well, Liss was not your run of the mill gal. Why he himself was surprised he found himself thinking about her. She was just a tomboy he kept telling himself, yet she had a way to get into one's soul and mind and well he had to admit she had eyes that looked into one's soul and wouldn't let go.

As he heads out of the office, he heads toward the telegraph office. His thought was to at least explain to Liss and her folks that he arrived safely at Fort Bennett and would be staying there for a while; how long he did not know. As he slowly walked out of the telegraph office, he wondered why e really sent that wire. Was it to let the judge know why he had not returned or was it a promise to let Liss know he had not forgotten her.

Later that evening, back in Washington in the back law office of Jacob Schummer, Mr. Schummer and a group of men had gathered. These men were six fine upstanding citizens of the community and were the investment backers of Mr. Carter and the other miners. These men were responsible for the men to bring the gold to them and supposedly to get their share, only that part never happened. Through a leak in the office of the secretary, Schummer's secretary was able to get a copy of the wire Captain Stiles sent for the miners being removed from the site.

Schummer looked up from his desk as the last man came in the office, "gentlemen, I called you all here to discuss a wire I received earlier today stating the government has given the railroad the rights to the land we had taken and Mr. Carter and his men are now guests at Fort Bennett awaiting further instructions. Now since there is no Golden Nugget Mining and never was one, so to speak of on file there are no funds for these unfortunate men. My only solution is to state I have no idea what this Mr. Carter is talking about. I furthermore will state, I had in good faith allowed Mr. Carter and his men to borrow a said amount to purchase land in the territory called Montana and to pay back the loan in monthly payments. I had idea he had taken the land under false pretenses and I future demand the initial loan be returned to me. Now, if we all are in agreement on this, I will send the wire out in the morning. Are there any objections?"

Schummer looked as a tall gentleman to Schmmer's left looks at him, "Jacob, what about our other ventures in other territories?"

Jacob looks up at him, "right now, I feel the others are safe we will continue with those ventures since they are here in the east. Well gentlemen, I believe this meeting is over, I thank you for coming."

With that, one by one the men leave the office and head off into the night.

David Osgood, Schummer's partner, looks at him as he closes the door, "what about the miners?"

"Oh I don't think we have to worry about them, after all, they are just men down and out who fought a war on the wrong side and like so many will never be able to get out of the hole they dug themselves in. I'm sure the army will send them on their way."

"What about the secretary?"

"What about him? Do you really think the new administration has the time or interest to follow a complaint by a group of Southerns, down and out drifters who still feel they were right? Good Lord Osgood, we won the war, not them! It's time they learned their way of life is a thing of the past and there it will remain."

It was early evening back in Montana, the Crawfords were coming back from town. It was the usual beginning of the month, shopping for supplies and the judge thought it would be a good move to have Liss join Jason this time, mainly he felt a change of scenery would perk her up a bit. As they quietly head the wagon home, Liss seems to be in a quiet mood.

Jason looks over to her, "you didn't seem to enjoy any of that chocolate cake earlier."

She looked at him and smiled, as long as she could remember he had always been there for her. Her big brother, her best friend, heck, there was nothing she couldn't talk to him about. Nothing until now.

"Did you enjoy yourself in town Liss?"

She looked down at the floor board of the wagon, "it was okay."

Seems she still wasn't the Liss he knew. "Maybe I can get Eli to let you join us with the horses, would you like that? I mean it's been a while since you've been out with all of us; the guys would love to see you."

She looks at him and smiles, "I know what you are doing and I really think it's sweet, but I'm fine. Honest!"

Jason smiled back at her, she really was a special gal. He then remembered the wire he was given before they left town. It was from Fort Bennett and addressed to the Circle C Ranch. He took it from his pocket and handed it to her. "Maybe this will make you feel better."

She looked at it. "It's probably for Papa."

"It's addressed to the Circle C and I believe you are part of the circle C."

She looked at him.

"Go ahead open it."

Slowly. she opened the envelope and unfolded the paper. She started to read it and began to smile and then began to read it aloud., "Dear Judge, hope this finds you well. I delivered my assignment here at the fort. I have been asked to remain here on another task that needs my help. When completed, I hope I can visit your ranch and spend some time with you and your family. Cully."

She closed her eyes and smiled. In that moment, Jason saw the Liss that he hadn't seen since Cully left. *Could it be our little tomboy is growing up? Could it be our Liss has found a man who had stolen her heart?* She looked at Jason, "do you think Papa would be upset?"

"For what?"

"Well, I read his wire,"

Jason smiled, "Sweetie, it's addressed to the Circle C and last time I looked, you are part of the Circle C. Besides I don't think your papa wouldn't mind at all, especially when he sees that pretty grin back in your face."

She leaned over and kissed his cheek, "you're the best Jason."

"So are you pretty one."

For the rest of the ride back to the ranch, Liss had a smile on her face.

## Chapter 3

Back at the fort, Cully was still trying to find a way to help the miners. There was a slim chance, but one he had to try. He decided to write a letter to his friend at the secretary's office in Washington and then to the man who had this dream of the railroad, Theodore Judah, a young engineer who first had the idea of running track through the mountain passes, not around them. True the railroad usually hired Chinese to lay track, but there was no reason to not hire a few strong and willing men from our own country wouldn't be possible. He knew Theodore even toyed with the idea of working for him a few years back, but Cully had a restless toe and sitting in one place for too long; well, it wasn't him. Either way it was worth a try; he wanted to help Nathaniel and his men.

For a moment, he tries to gather his words and at that moment Liss entered his thoughts.

It also was the time Doug walked into the mess hall. He sees Cully in the back corner and starts to walk over. Cully didn't even see him walk up and sit down. "Hey there."

Cully looks at him, "hey."

Doug looks at him, "Okay, the only time I've seen you preoccupied she was either blond, brunette, or a red head. So tell me, which is she?"

Cully looked, not really hearing what he said, still trying to write this letter, "she who?"

Doug smiled, "the gal who has you off in some dream world."

"Look Doug, I'm trying to find some work for Nathaniel and his men and if you have any ideas I could use them."

"Well can they work as ranch hands? Maybe that judge you know can use help. You said he was getting his herd ready for roundup."

Cully looked at Doug and smiled, "Doug, you are the best. I'll be right back." With that he gets up and heads out the door. He headed to the telegraph office, a smile on his face, maybe just maybe, he'd be back at the Circle C before he knew it.

Cully made his way across the yard and to the small cabin near the stable where Carter and his men had been placed for now. It was a bit tight, but the men were thankful for it since the last year they had been sleeping under the stars. It was here Cully approached them with the idea of working at the Circle C, until he could reach the railroad.

Carter looked at Cully, "let me ask you this Son, if'in we like this ranchin', is there a chance we kin stay on and be a workin there fir a spell? I mean at least until we kin get a place of our own?"

"Well I suppose it could be worked out, but let's just see what we have to work with for now."

The old man smiles at him, "Son, you are a good friend; I thank you for all your help."

"My pleasure Mr. Carter. I can't promise you anything, but Judge Crawford is a decent man and will find a way to help all of you get what's owed you."

He looked at the man, "by the way, you can ride, can't you?"

The old man smiles at him, "you want to tell me what Southern boy do't? Why we learned to ride afore we could walk."

They both smiled. "We'll be moving on as soon as I get an answer from the judge."

"We won't forget you Son."

With that, Cully leaves the cabin and walks towards his cabin. As he walks in the door, his mind brings up the image of Liss. True, he did want to get back to her, he was also hoping the good judge would be able to help Carter and his men until more suitable employment could be obtained. He made his way to the desk and sat down, hoping to get started on the letters when Doug came into the room holding in his hands a tray of food.

"I took it for granted that you didn't eat and I can't have one of my men starving and…"

"You know you're crazy don't you?"

He looked at Cully, "I know, but I, also, know that you've got something in that head of yours. So what is it?"

"Well I got to thinking 'bout what Carter said and how they was working for this mining company back east and how they been working here for some time and gave all their money back east only to be told their jobs were over. I figured I'd send a wire to the railroad and ask if they could use some experienced men who knew the mountains well and then I thought maybe Judge Crawford could use some extra ranch hands for round up."

Doug looks a Cully and smiles, "I see, as I recall, the good judge has a far size spread and I do remember he has a young gal; should be about sixteen or seventeen by now." Doug looks at him, "is that who she is?"

Cully takes the coffee cup from the tray and takes a sip, "Doug, you're jumping to conclusions as always."

Doug sees the look on his face, "you can't fool me old friend. Tell me, is she a pretty young thing?"

His mind went to his memory of her and the look on his face answered Doug's question.

"Well that does it, if the judge okays the idea, I will be more than happy to give you a full military escort back to the Circle C."

"I really don't think that will be necessary."

"Oh but I insist and as an appointed officer to watch over all in this territory, it's my duty to see these miners are to be taken to the Circle C with full military escort."

"Have you forgotten these men have been on their own in the mountains for over a year now?"

"But now they are on a military fort and are entitled to full protection."

It was the next morning, Cully set his mind up and sent the wire to the judge; as he came out of the telegraph office, he noticed a crowd gathered toward the front gate and the rider who just rode in. It was a young man from a near-by farm; seems they had raid at their home last evening.

When Cully got there, the young Johnny Cummings was telling the story to Doug, "They came down from the hills Sir. I ain't never seen anything like it before. They killed my mamma's good milk cow before they left." Doug looked at the boy who couldn't be much older than twelve."

"Your ma and pa, are they alright?"

"Yes sir, my mama said for me to ride here and tell yall, just in case they head for another farm.:

Doug looked at Cully, "Cully take a small group of men and follow this young lad back to his farm, just in case those Indians head back."

"Captain, do you think…"

Doug looks at him, "Do you suggest I send this young boy back alone and as I see it, unarmed to face whatever he comes in contact with until he reaches his farm?"

"No, I'm sorry Sir."

Within a short time the young boy and Cully and a small group of troopers left the fort and are on their way back to the boy's farm. They arrived at the farm only to find the boy's family were killed. The horses were gone and the tracks showed the Indians went back into the hills. His instinct told him to follow, yet he had the boy to think of, so they headed back to the fort and report what happened to Captain Stiles.

Martin Reynolds looked at Cully, "Sir, don't you think we should go after the enemy?"

"Corporal. Sometimes one has to retreat in order to gain victory at another time. Our main concern now is to get Johnny back to the fort and notify his next of kin."

"But Sir, doesn't it make us look like we ran?"

Cully looks at the boy, "Corporal, we just laid to rest this boy's folks and I kinda like to think they'd want us to take care of this young one and get him to safety."

"Yes sir."

"Martin, don't worry, we're not running, just waiting for another time, another place."

The boy smiles and head toward his horse.

They arrived back at the fort in the early afternoon and Cully had Martin get the Johnny settled before returning to Cully's office, it was Doug who was waiting for Cully to hear his report.

Cully opens his office door and sees Doug, "Well I must say this is getting to be a habit with you."

Doug gets up from the chair, "skip the small talk; what happened?"

Slowly Cully walks to his desk, "well do you want the long story with all the hearts and flowers or the short version?"

"Skip the jokes Cully, what happened?"

"Well we got to the farm, both the boy's parents were killed along with his older brother. The took the horses and headed off up into the hills."

Doug asks, "and you didn't follow?"

"My main concern was to give this boy's family a decent burial and get him back here to safety."

"So am I to understand you left these savages to kill and raid another farm while you and the men dug graves?"

He looked at Doug, "Sir, I felt my duty was to give these folks a decent final resting place and to get their only surviving son to safety. If I was wrong, then so be it, but I felt I owed his parents to get him to safety!"

Doug looked down for a moment, then back up at Cully, "Yes, I suppose you are right."

"If you would permit me, I would like to send a wire to young Master Cumming's aunt in Denver of what happened and assure her that her nephew would be on his way to her as soon as she confirms the wire."

Doug looks at him and shakes his head, "I have to admit you did the right thing; seems that you've grown up."

"Is this the part where you tell me what a great future I'll have in this man's army? If it is, do spare me; I'd rather face a firing squad."

Doug looks at him, "Oh I can arrange that if you like."

Cully shakes his head and walks out and slams the door.

The news of the Indian raids to the north reached The Circle C and the neighboring ranches. Though there had been no sightings in the past years; the fact that the prospectors going into the mountains and breaking the treaty did not make matters easy.

With the death of Spirit Moon, the chief of the tribe, the younger braves were in favor of breaking the treaty and raiding, not only the miners, but the neighboring ranches and taking the cattle. Their people were starving and the fact that the buffalo herds were dwindling; thanks to the hunters who killed the animals only for the hides; leaving the meat to rot in the hot sun.

True the Cummings' farm was closer to the fort, but that didn't stop the raiding of all ranches fifteen years ago, before any treaty was even established and signed. A good many ranchers remembered the raids and the death and destruction across the whole territory. It was a young boy who was able to speak with the war council back then. A young boy whose great grandmother had taught him the ways of her people and his rightful place to address them. It had been a long time since he had ventured back to the land of his great grandmother's people. A long time since the young boy with eyes as blue as a clear morning sky chose to walk the path of both people. It was the, main reason he was chosen for the mission to get the miners out.

The day had just started at the Circle C and already most of the ranch hands had already left for the range to get started on the branding.

In his study. the judge sat at his desk when Liss walks in with a wire from Fort Bennett.

"This just came in Papa."

"Thank you Liss," he opens the envelope and begins to read, looking up, he smiles at her, "It's from Mr. Cully!"

"Cully! Does he say when he's coming back? Is everything …"

The judge puts his hand up for her to stop with the questions, "Well if you can control yourself for a moment I can tell you. He states he's still at the fort, he wants to know if I need some hands to help here at the ranch."

"That's it? He doesn't ask anything else?"

The judge looks at the wire, then back to her, "no, nothing else. You have to remember Liss. it's a wire, not a five page letter."

She looks down, disappointed he didn't mention her and she was hurt.

The judge looks at her and hands her the wire, "if you like, you can read it."

She looks at him and just shakes her head no and walks out of the room. He watches her leave, it's hard for him to picture his little girl was growing up. The little girl who was at his side all the time had found someone new she wanted to be with. He now was just daddy, not her hero anymore.

He was lost in his thoughts and didn't see his wife walk in. She looks at him knowing his thoughts are so many miles away. Gently she pats his shoulder, "day dreaming?"

He smiles at her, "Liz, I'm afraid our little girl is growing up?"

"Growing up? Where have you been my dear husband? She's not growing, she's grown up and from what've seen she's picked herself out a beau."

He looked at her, "a beau?"

She smiles at him and nods.

A smile comes to the judge's face as he thinks about having another male around the ranch. Why it might be just the perfect thing to sit back and let the young ones run the place. As he smiled at the idea, it hit him that maybe Mr. Cully may not feel the same way about his Liss. "Are we sure this Cully is interested in Liss?"

"Eli, sometimes I wonder how you ever got to be a judge. Didn't you see the way he looked at her? I tell you he even stayed an extra day here just to be with her.'"

Eli smiled and took her hand in his, "you know Elizabeth, I looked at you the same way when I first met you. I still do." He gently places a kiss on her hand.

She smiles and places a kiss on his forehead, "oh I knew that the moment I met you, I was wondering how long you would take to ask my papa for my hand."

"Well to tell ya the truth your pa did scare me."

"Papa? Well that's silly, he was always so very fond of you."

"Fond of the young lawyer in his firm; not the potential husband of his only daughter."

She walked toward the window and saw Jason coming to the door. "Well he was wrong and you not only became a successful lawyer and judge, but a wonderful husband to me and father to Liss."

As Jason walks into the room she smiles and walks out. "Morning Jason."

"Morning Mz. Crawford."

Eli looks at his foreman, "well ready to get those cows branded?"

Jason smiles and looks at him. "You know Judge, so far the only other hands that signed up for the branding are the boys from the Lazy S."

"Can you tell me why or am I to guess?"

Jason looks at him, "why you know why Judge. It's those dang Injins and the raiding they are doing."

Eli gets up from his chair, "you mean to tell me these ranchers are letting a few Injins burning one farm stop the entire roundup and branding of the calves? What fool headed idiot put that idea in their heads?"

Jason looks at him, "well Sir, it was Captain Stiles' wire he sent and he stated that all ranchers should get a copy."

"Get a copy? Good Lord, doesn't that solider boy realize that raid was over sixty miles from here? I tell you this Yankee soldiers just don't understand out here; ya'll can't always find the answers in those school books they gives you back in the day."

"Sir, you have to understand they are worried for their families and when the captain offered to give them shelter at the fort, they took it."

Eli looked at him, "and you, do you think I'm stupid to stay and keep Liz and Liss here?"

"Sir, I know you know what you're doing and I, also, know you would move heaven and hell to make sure Liss and Mz. Crawford are safe. Does that answer your question?"

He smiles at him, the man had come a long way from the boy he met by the stream those many years ago.

At this point, Liss comes in the study in her usual smiling self. She nods at Jason, then Eli.

He looks at her, "and where do you think you're going Melissa?"

She looked at Jason, who just bows his head. He has no idea what she's done, but it had to be something cause her pa didn't call her by her given name without a good reason. "Well are you going to answer me!"

"I… I just came in to say good morning Papa."

He looked at her, knowing he had upset her for no reason. "Well good morning and make sure you stay close to the ranch."

She was about to ask a question when Jason shook his head.

Eli looked at him, "I'll expect you and the men with the herd and get the branding started. One more thing only brand our calves."

"Yes sir." He turns and smiles at Liss as he leaves.

A while later, Jason is on the range and with the tally book in his hand marking the calves that are Circle C's as the young ones are being branded. He looks up and sees Jim Wallace riding up. Jim was foreman for the Lazy M Ranch owned by Adam Miller.

The Miller spread was a good size not as big as the Circle C, yet it held its own with the others. He gets off his horse, smiles and walks over to Jason, "well looks like they got you doing the easy work there Boy."

Jason looks up from the ledger, "well I was just beginning to wonder where ole Jim Wallace could be. He' s never late for a roundup."

"Well see Son, it's this way, my boss is not gonna be doing any branding this year."

Jason looks at him, "would mind telling me why or do you want me to guess?"

Jim looks at him, "mind if we walk a bit?"

Jason hands the ledger to the ranch hand and directs Jim to the chuck wagon. "I'll buy you a cup of cookie's coffee."

Jim looks at him, "is it still strong and bitter?"

"Yep."

Sitting on the other end of the campfire, Jim explains the reason the Lazy M boys are missing.

"Well tell ya the truth, I was kinda thinking that. Seems quite a few of you folks are taking Captain Stiles' offer. But do you think the Sioux are gonna come this far down and raid our cattle?"

"You meaning to tell me that Adam Miller really thinks those…"

Jim stops him. "it ain't him, it's the missus. Ever since she heard about that poor Cummings family and then the wire from that Captain Stiles inviting everyone to the fort for protection, well you see he's outnumbered."

Jason looks at him, "well can't really blame her. I mean they have six youngins."

"Seven!"

"Seven?"

"Yep, Mrs. Miller had another boy 'bout six months ago."

Jason smiles, "at the rate he's going ole'Adam will have all his sons as his ranch hands.'"

"Well that be the missus' fault, she keeps saying she'd like a gal."

Jason smiles, "and Adam is trying to please her there too it seems." Jason takes a sip of his coffee, then empties his cup to the side of him, "one day cookie is gonna make a decent pot of coffee…"

Jim stops him before he can finish, "but not today." He laughs and they both head toward the horses. Jim looks at Jason, "well I best being getting back to Mr. Miller."

"Yea, and I've got to tell the judge the news."

They smile and head off in different directions.

## Chapter 4

Eli was sitting on the front porch when Jason came riding up.

He smiled at Eli, "Afternoon Judge."

Eli nodded, "working half a day Son?"

Jason gets down off the horse, "no Sir, it's just I figured it would be best if I told you this."

Eli didn't like the sound of that so he gets up and walks into the house and toward his study with Jason behind him. He walks into the room and Jason follows closing the door. As he sits down at his desk, he looks at Jason, "well?"

"Well Sir, it seems we won't have boys from the Lazy M to help with the branding."

"And that is because?"

"Well Sir, Mr. Miller is taking his family to Fort Bennett until this whole Sioux uproar is ended."

"You mean to tell me, Adam Miller is gonna turn tail and run?"

"Well Sir, it isn't him. It's the misses. She heard about the Cumming's and what happened to them and she doesn't want to see the same happen to her kids."

Eli looks at him, "how did this whole news of the Cummings' come about?"

"The wire that I gave you last week, it seems a copy was given to all the ranchers out here. Seems this Captain Stiles offered every farmer and rancher the protection of the fort."

Eli got up from his chair, "and you mean to tell me these yellow lily-livered cowboys as they like to think they are deciding to run and hide behind the ivory walls of the mighty Fort Bennett? Them walls are not ivory, but wood and they aren't the walls of Jericho which if I recall from my Bible came a tumbling down also. And who do these cattlemen, and I use that term loosely think is going to brand their calves? Not my drovers."

Jason looks at him, "I'm not taking their side, but you know how the women folk get when they hear war party."

Eli looks at him, "war party or not, if they don't show up to brand their calves, leave them. I will not have my men do any other ranch hands job."

Jason knew better than to stop Eli when he was on a rant.

"Good Lord, I remember when Adam and Claire came out here to this territory. Why they were a nice young couple; had a young boy. Adam had his heart set on making a life for his family here. What could have made Claire want to leave?"

Jason looked at him, "they do have a passel of youngins. I heard that Mrs. Miller just had another one, not more than six months ago."

Eli looked at him and shook his head, "yeah, well I guess that would be a powerful reason to pick up and leave."

Jason looked at him. He knew how much the ranch meant to him, but he also knew that Liz and Liss meant more.

Eli looked out the window of his study where Liz and Liss were sitting. "Like I said. I can understand his reason."

Jason nods, "yes Sir, I hear ya."

Back at the fort, the wagon loads of settlers were arriving each day. There was hardly a space for another wagon, yet in they came.

Cully looked at Carter, Morning Sir, it seems it's getting a bit crowded here."

Carter looks at him, "It seems everyone is running for cover, afraid we're gonna be out of room at the rate these folks are coming in."

Suddenly, Corporal Reynolds sees them and walks over to them. "Mr. Cully, Mr. Cully, Captain Stiles asks that you see him in his office as soon as possible."

Cully smiles at the boy, "alright Marty, take it easy, the captain can wait a few minute. Hey didn't I tell you, you can call me Cully, don't need to put a Mr. in front of the name."

The boy smiles, Cully is the only one who ever showed any kindness to him. "Yes sir."

"No sir either, ya hear me?"

"Yes Si… Cully."

Cully smiles, "there ya go." He looks at Carter, "I reckon I best be going to see what Doug wants. I'll meet up with later, if it's alright."

Carter smiles and nods, he had come to like the boy; he was a fine young man.

Cully also found he did want to help them. He turns to Martin, "Okay Marty, let's go see what ole' Doug wants."

The boy smiles as he leads the way to the captain's office.

Captain Stiles looks at Cully as he walks into his office. "You wanted to see me Doug?"

The captain looks at the corporal and the young boy leaves the room. "Cully, I sent for you because I frankly I have no one else I can depend on for this."

"Well if it's the miners, I sent a wore out to Judge Crawford if he was willing to give these men a job until we can work something out with the railroad."

"That's not it. Cully, I need someone I can trust to go into those mountains and speak with the Sioux to let the railroad go in there and lay track."

Cully walked over to the chair and sat down, "now let me get this straight, you want me to ride up into the hills and tell, not ask, but tell the Sioux to let the railroad lay down track for the train that will pass through their land? Is this what you're saying?"

"Well you are…"

Cully gets up from the chair. "Now Doug, we've been friends for a long time and I did you solider boys a favor by going and getting the miners for ya, but if ya think I'm going up there and tell the Sioux they have to let you run track across their burial grounds. I told Theodore Judah some time back when he asked me the same deal; I may be a bit touched in the head, but not touched. I ain't ready to meet my maker just yet, I stll have a good deal of living to do. You do remember what happened to the last army boy who tried to do that, don't ya? You remember he was called the yellow-haired wonder of the civil war!"

Doug looks at him, "that was a different set of circumstances."

"But they all never did make it out did they?"

Doug looked at him, "look I'll even let you take the miners with you. After all, they know the trails."

"Doug, I am not taking anyone up there and I'm not going. I'll be leaving in the morning, I'm a bit overdue for a visit."

He gets up and is about to leave when Doug sarcastically says, "don't be surprised if that young gal you're so interested in isn't there. You know how those savages are; they will strike anywhere; they don't follow plans."

He looks at him, "well I'll just have to see for myself then." With that he opens the door and walks out of the office and heads for the cabin the miners had.

Doug walks out of his office and looks at the corporal, "send a wire to General Grover, tell him Callhan refuses his request."

Cully looked out the window of his room and wondered why the railroad was so insistent on the route going through the mountain, after all everyone knew the pass would be useless once the snow fell. At times the pass was blocked for months; many a trapper was stuck up there and many died with the bitter cold. No, there was something else they wanted, but what was it? They already knew about the gold, so there wasn't it. What could it be?

He had known Doug for a good many years, at least since the war, even though they were on opposite sides believing they were right. But it was Doug who convinced the top brass that Cully was the only one who could get the Sioux to agree to their terms, being his lineage. He didn't understand that Cully didn't regard his grandmother's people as savages and his regard of the white men over the years made him wonder who truly were the savages. They rose early and Cully wasted no time in getting his saddlebags packed and he headed for the stable to get his horse.

To his surprise, he found waiting there for him Carter and his men. "Morning, Mr. Cully. We thought it would be a nice day to take a ride. Would you mind if we all rode along with you?"

He looks at the man, "well, tell ya the truth I wouldn't mind the company, but I can't say you'll be findin' work there; I never did get an answer from the judge."

Carter smiles, "let's just let us worry 'bout that. 'Sides it was getting a bit crowded at the fort."

Cully nods and smiles, "I hear ya there."

They mount up and slowly make their way out of the fort gates.

Eli made his way to the window in his study and gazed across the ranch and the stable. It seemed nothing was going as planned and now along with the Lazy M, two more ranches had decided to pack up and head to the fort for protection. It's hard for Eli to understand why. These men were all fine hard working ranchers come out to this territory to find a new life for themselves and their families. And though they had their lives here in this valley; the safety of their families right now was most on their minds. Slowly, he made his way out of the study and into the kitchen where he sees Liss smiling at him.

"Hi Papa, ready for some breakfast?"

He smiles at her, "if I can sit down across the table from a pretty gal like you, I surely am ready."

He gently squeezes her arm and heads for the opposite side of the table and sits down. He looks at the platter on the table and smiles. "Well, what have we here?"

Liss smiles at him, "there's bacon, sausage, of course eggs and...'"

He stops her, "I think I'll settle for just eggs and toast."

She looks at him and was about to say something when Jason walked in the back door. "Morning folks."

Liss smiles at him. "Morning Jason.

He leans down and kisses her cheek, how's my favorite girl this morning?"

She looks up and smiles at him, "Just fine. Would you like some breakfast?"

She hands him a cup of coffee, "thanks Sweetie," He looks at Eli, "sir, if it's not too much I'd like to speak with you." Eli gets up from his chair and both men head to the study. Jason closes the door behind them and then turns to Eli.

"Alright what seems to be the problem?"

He looks at the judge, "well Sir, you know I wouldn't ask this if we were not short-handed.'"

Eli nodded, but still has no idea what the problem is.

"Well Sir, I need three of your men here; seems a good stretch of fence on the east range has gone down. Now I ain't saying it was torn down or cut, but if we don't get it back up, we're gonna be chasing strays until we're ready to take the herd to the freight yards."

Eli looks at him, he knows the boy is right, he also knows he wouldn't ask if they weren't shorthanded. "I see your point, take Paco, Pete and Seth and let me know why that fence is down."

Jason smiled and started to head out the door when Eli stopped him, "One more thing tell your favorite girl out there good bye; you know she gets upset when you don't."

He smiles at him. "Yes Judge."

You will let me know on that fence, right?"

As Jason walks out the door she smiles, "yes Sir."

Eli shakes his head and smiles as he walks back over to his desk. He had to admit he was fond of Jason and well, he'd think about that at another time, his Liss was still too young to be serious. He lit a match; he was about to light his pipe when Liz walked in.

"I take it you'll not be having anymore breakfast?"

He looked at her and knew there was something more on her mind, "alright Liz, what's on that mind of yours?"

"Well, I was just thinking, do you think maybe we should pack up and head for the fort?"

He looked at her, "do you want us to go? If you feel it's the right move, I'll start packing."

She looked at him. He knew as well as he, this ranch was not just home it was their dreams, their hopes… everything they had ever wanted and dreamed of was here. Liss was born on this ranch. She looks out the window, "I don't know what to think Eli. What if the fence didn't happen to fall what if…"

Eli stops her, "now Liz, we 've dealt with this before and we never ran."

She knew he was right, they had dealt with Indian raids in the past, this was not the time to run. Besides there were no signs of any Sioux in the area. She smiled at Eli and headed for the door when she heard his voice,

"I promise you if I see any trouble, I'll get you and Liss out of here."

Slowly, she turns and smiles at him, "I know Eli."

As Liz enters the kitchen, she sees Liss standing at the window by the sink. As she slowly moves, she sees Jason moving up to join the other ranch hands.

"Are you also not eating breakfast?"

Liss slowly turns and reaches for the cup in the counter, "no I was just getting a cup to have some coffee." She walks over to the table and Liz looks down at the cup of coffee near her daughter's dish. "Well, it is best to have a fresh cup, after all you do want a hot cup of coffee."

Liss turned a bit pink with embarrassment. "Yes, it is best hot."

She looks toward the back door and Liz looks at her, "You do remember your father said no one was allowed to leave the ranch."

She looks at her mother, "but I was only going to…" She sees there was no way she'll get past the door. Slowly, she turns and heads back to the table and begins turning the food on her plate with her fork.

## Chapter 5

In Washington D.C., in the office of Jacob Schummer, six men have gathered around the large table. Six men who have been wondering what indeed happened to the funds they were to receive from the now terminated. Miners. It was all agreed on that the gold from that mine in the Montana Territory would be sent to the bank in San Francisco. What they didn't know was Schummer took the money; theirs as well as his and invested it into another venture that never really happened. It was a business that would funding businesses in the San Francisco area, it was a sure fire way to double their money. Why just the profits on the lumber business alone would bring in a profit. What Schummer didn't plan on was earthquakes. Within a matter of minutes, an entire fortune and dreams was gone crumbled into the ground.

It was Abe Levy, a shy gentle man, who was the local tailor in town. He and his wife Sofie came to this county from Germany like so many others with a dream to have a better life and though things were good, it didn't hurt to have a little stored away for the day Abe wouldn't able to work anymore. It wasn't to get rich. it was to be able in another fifteen years to maybe sit back and enjoy life. Slowly, Jacob looked around the room and at the faces of these men. How could he tell them that because of him, their money was gone. What was to keep them from taking him outside to the nearest tree and hanging him. Slowly, he rose from his chair and clearing his throat, he began his story and that's just what it was a tall story.

"I suppose you're wondering why I called you here and well, it's about this wire I got early this morning. It's from the president of the San Francisco bank. It seems there was an earthquake there yesterday and most of the city was destroyed. The bank was completely destroyed and it will take months before it can used again, thousands of dollars lost in the fire and rubble."

From the other side of the room the voice of Ralph Morganstern could be heard, "so we are to believe we believed in you and all our money is lost? All our money that we worked for is now gone! How could you do this to us Jacob?"

Jacob looks at him and the others, "need I remind you all; I lost my money also! We can't sit in sorrow for what has passed, but look to rebuild and start ..."

Slowly, the men get up from their seats and headed for the door and Jacob tries one last effort to stop them. "Gentlemen, let's sit down and talk about this calmly..."

He saw it was no use, they were heading out the door. He looks at the lone gentleman who remained, Cyrus Lane. Jacob looked at him, "well Cyrus, I did try."

He smiled and looked at Jacob, "you lied your way out of many a schemes, but this one was near on the best.

You never did put that money in the bank; you took it and bought your partnership on a scheme for yourself, didn't you?"

"You heard me, I said...."

"This is not a simple minded storekeeper you talking to Jacob. Why I've known you since you were able to pull your first deal, some twenty years ago. You never did send that money to the bank; you used it didn't you?"

"Sure I did I ..."

The old man looks at him and smiles, "you stole from all these people who trusted you. You took the money and if these fine folks knew what you did, why you could just be saying your prayers 'cause they'd hang you from the nearest tree."

Jacob looked at him as he pulled out his gun from the inside of his jacket, "that's why we aren't telling them anything right?"

"And what makes you so sure on that?"

Slowly, he cocks his gun, "because my ole' friend, if you don't agree, we can and will end this friendship right here and now."

Cyrus looks at him, "you wouldn't dare!"

Jacob gives him a sinister smile, "would you care to bet on that?"

Cyrus gets up from the chair, and heads to the door and steps into the street and into the darkness of the night.

Alone in his office, Jacob gets up and walks to the window and peers out into the empty street. Slowly, a dark figure walks into the room, walks to the table and picks up Jacob's gun and fires three shots into Jacob's body.

The second shot catches his chest as he turns and sees his killer just at the time, the third and fatal shot hits his chest directly to his heart.

The gunman places the gun back the gun back on the table and rushes out of the room and disappears into the darkness.

From the surrounding buildings, folks had rushed out to see what the noise was about.

William Harrelson, the night watchman for the hotel across the street, heard the shots and came running over. Slowly, he makes his way into Jacob's office and sees the body of Jacob in the pale moonlight slumped in the corner of the room. He walks over to the body and sees he was indeed shot three times and the kill shot would probably be the one in his chest. He turned his head and asked for someone to get Doc Clark.

Though it would be easier just to take Jacob to the undertaker; rules stated the body had to be certified dead by a physician. One of those silly rules the town officials had voted on last election.

Slowly, the doc made his way in the office and over to Bill. "Hey Doc, sorry to bring you out at this late hour but…"

James Clark had been the doctor for the town for as long as a body could remember. He looked at Bill, "they got you working the late shift again Bill?"

"Well, just till Jess gets back. They'd been making us work sixteen hour shifts…"

"Well it won't be too much longer, Jess and Cathy will be back from their honeymoon on Friday."

The doctor smiled, "I tell ya I never thought Cathy would ever get him to ask her."

Bill smiled, "everyone knew she was stuck on him since they were in grade school."

The doc looks up at him. "Okay Bill, let's get Jacob out of here and close the place up 'till morning."

Jacob Schummer was laid to rest in the town burial plot that afternoon while his business associates and friends attended. There was still no idea who shot him or why his gun was on the table.

Back in Montana, Jason and the hands had reached the north and the downed fence. It was oblivious it was no accident the fence was cut, by who and why were still the questions unanswered.

Jason was about to head for the wagon when he sees Cully riding toward him. "Well, if you ain't a sight for sore eyes."

Cully smiles at him, "I did tell ya I was coming back." Cully looks at Carter, then back to Jason, "Jason, this here is my friend Montgomery Carter and his friends. They were part of the miners that had to leave the hills, when all this frackus with the railroad came up."

Jason nods to Carter and the others, as Cully continues, "they came with me hoping they could find some work down here. Seems the outfit they was working for closed down and took the money with them." Jason looks at the men, he did need men, but do they have any knowledge about ranching. "I tell ya,, the judge could really use the help, we're short now and there's the branding," he looks at the men, "do any of you men know about ranching?"

Carter was the first to respond, "we're all from farm land back home Mr. Jason, each of us grew up and worked the family farms and ranches."

Jason smiled, "fine, I know I can speak for the judge and hire you right now."

The men all smiled and Carter noticed the downed fence. "You seem to have run into a problem here with your fence Mr. Jason. Would you allow me to show you an easier way to mend it?"

"No, not at all and it's just Jason to all of you."

Carter smiled and got off his horse and walked over to the fence. He went back to his horse and took out a clamp from his saddle bag, then walked back to the fence, only this time, Jason and Cully followed. Carter took a piece of the cut fence and made a loop slowly he threaded the wire through and clamped it, then wrapping it around the post, he pulled the entire wire taut and then clamped it to the fence. He smiled at Jason, "that will be holding it for ya.'"

Jason looked closer and smiled, "Mr. Carter, that is a fine piece fine work."

"Thank you Jason, but it's just Carter, no need for mister. If it's alright with you Jason, my men and I would like to rebuild the rest of this fence, I can see that it could use a bit of tightening."

Jason looks at him, "by all means Carter you're hired."

They shook hands and the miners got off their horses and followed Carter to the fence.

Jason looked back at Cully, "well, guess you'll be headin' to the ranch?"

"I could stay here, but then again, I think one of us should tell the judge he has some new ranch hands.'"

Jason nods, "with the way things were going, we were gonna wait or the branding."

"I noticed, where's all the other hands?"

"With all the talk of the Sioux raiding. most of the ranchers here picked up and took their families to the fort. Seems no one wants to stay around."

"The judge is still here."

Jason smiles at him, "do you really think some Indians gonna make the judge run?"

Cully had to agree, the judge he knew was not one to run. Cully smiles and made his way down the trail. He looked forward to seeing the judge, but, also, to see Liss. He could almost see her sitting on the porch since the judge wouldn't let her leave the ranch. Maybe she wouldn't be so happy to see him. After all he was free to come and go and she well…"

Back at the Circle C, Liss and her mother sat on the porch enjoying the afternoon sun as they kept themselves busy with their needlepoint. Well, Liz kept herself busy, she never really got the hang of the art of needlepoint or to put it bluntly, she didn't want to learn something so dumb as that, she called it. Oh, Liz tried numerous times to explain the process, but Liss just wasn't interested.

It was just another afternoon as the Crawford ladies sat on the porch, until Liss happened to look up and see a rider headed toward the house. She got up for a closer look. *Could it be? Was it?* A smile came to her face as she rushed off the porch steps and ran to the rider who had now dismounted his horse and was standing there waiting for her. She runs into his arms and he hugs her and she's just so happy to see him.

"You're back! Oh I can't believe you're back!"

He smiles at her, "I told ya I'd be back."

She hugs him again, "I can't believe…"

He places his arm around her waist as they walked back toward the porch where Liz still sat waiting and smiling. "It's so good to see you Cully."

He smiled at her, "a pleasure to see you, Mz. Crawford."

"Please do sit down," she looks at Liss, "Melissa, tell your father Mr. Cully is here. Mr. Cully, can I get you anything to drink?"

Cully shakes his head, "no thanks Mz, Crawford, I really came to talk to the judge."

As Liz is about to get up. Eli rushes out the door and grabs Cully by the shoulders. "Cully, it's so good to see you. I was just wondering when you'd be coming back our way. Why I was even telling Liz yesterday, I wonder when Cully will stop back." He places his arm on his shoulder, "I'd love to hear 'bout your trip, shall we go into the study?"

They walk back into the house and leave Liz and Liss on the porch.

Liss looks at her mother, "what just happened?"

Liz shakes her head and smiles, "we've just became unimportant and not needed until supper time." Liz puts her arm around Liss' shoulder as they head into the house.

In the judge's study, Cully explains the problems throughout the area that farmers, as well as ranchers were having with the Sioux.

Eli seemed to understand the problem was affecting the entire territory, but the military can't seem to control or keep the Sioux under control. He, also, knew that because of this problem he had no other ranch hands to help with the branding, which is already behind schedule.

Cully looks at him, "I explained in the wire I sent you last month asking if you needed some hands."

"Wire? I didn't get any wire."

Suddenly Liss walks into the room. "Liss, do you know anything about a wire from Cully that came last month?"

She lowers her head and began to talk in a low voice, "Jason said I could open it and it didn't seem too important and it was from Cully, so I saw he said he was coming back so I just…"

"Melissa Gabriella Christina Crawford…"

Before her father could finish, she ran out of the room and up the stairs.

Eli looks at Cully, "I'm sorry, I had no idea …"

Cully smiles, "It's me who's sorry Sir. I should have addressed the wire to you personally."

Eli smiled, "just for my own curiosity, what was in this mysterious wire?"

Cully smiled, "it was a simple request; if you could use some extra hands on the ranch and of course hoping you all were doing all right. "

"Extra hands?"

"Yes sir, these gentlemen that were working the mines were closed down by their company and left them with no wages after working for nearly eight months. I was hoping you might need some help around the ranch. They'd be mighty beholden to you."

"I'd be beholden to them; we have no ranch hands to help with the branding as I told you."

Suddenly, Liss comes back into the room and hands her pa the wire. She looks at Cully who gives her a smile and she smiles back.

Eli looks ay Cully, "it's like you said, so I'll tell you again, I'd be happy to hire them."

"Thank you Sir, I'll go tell the men; I left them back with Jason.

He heads out the door as Liss follows him; they get to the front porch as she watches him get on his horse.

He looks down at her and smiles, "Dang, I forgot how pretty you are. Remind me to tell you that later." He leans down and kisses her cheek, then turns and rides off.

Liz walks out and sees Liss standing on the porch swaying side to side. "I can see you're happy he's back."

She turns an smiled at her mother. "Happy, oh Mama, he said I was pretty! He said he dang near forgot how pretty I was! Can you believe it Mama?" She took her mother's arm and twirled around the porch as they were at a dance.

"Liss slow down."

She smiles at her mother, "did you hear me Mama?"

Eli comes out hearing all the noise and sees them dancing on the porch. Is there something for such jocularity?"

Liz slowly sits in a nearby chair as Liss continues to dance, she grabs her father's hand, "isn't it wonderful Papa, he thinks I'm pretty.?:

Eli looks at his wife who mouths Cully's name to him. Eli smiles and it all becomes clear.

Liss looks at him, "you do like him Papa, oh please say you do?"

Eli caught off guard, "yes I think he's a fine young man."

She stops dancing and hugs her father, "oh Papa, I knew you'd like him."

Eli stops to catch his breath and looks at his daughter, still dancing. It was at that moment he realized his little girl wasn't a little girl anymore. No longer would he be seeing that scrawny little tomboy follow the ranch hands around the ranch and trying to race Jason to the south fence and back. He wondered *when did it happen? When did she become a woman?*

Liz looks at her husband and seeing the look on his face knows what he's thinking. "Eli, she's seventeen years old, the little girl you knew has grown up and what you see dancing is Miss Melissa Crawford."

Eli looks at her, it was gonna take some getting used to, but it was something he'd have to face.

Back on the north range, Cully finds Jason and the men herding the cattle back through the fence.

Jason smiles as he sees Cully ride up. "What's the word from the judge?"

Cully looks at them, "you got yourself some fine ranch hands.'"

Carter smiles at Cully, "I'm beholden to you Son."

"It was nothing, besides both of you made out well, you got the job and the judge gets his steers branded."

Jason looks at him, "and you get to see a young lady who is probably sitting on the porch waiting for your return."

Cully lowers his head to hide his smile, "Guess we'd better get these steers back behind the fence and head for the bunk house." He looks at Jason, then the cows, "let's get going."

It was late afternoon with the hands, along with Jason and Cully ride up to the bunkhouse. "I'll go up and tell the judge we'll start the branding in the morning. Is there anything you'd like to say to a certain young lady?"

Cully lowers his head and smiles, "no, that's quite alright, but thank you for asking."

Jason pats his back and heads up to the main house.

Carter looks at Cully, "if you want to go and see the young lady, why don't let me and the boys…"

" Before he could finish Cully stops him."

"Carter, I appreciate your… Well let's just get you and the guys settled inside."

It was Liss who greeted Jason at the door thinking he was someone else. With a big smile on her face that faded as she saw Jason standing there.

Hi beautiful, is the judge in his study?"

"Yes." She was somewhat confused. but held the door open for Jason as he walked in.

Jason smiled, "he's at the bunkhouse with the new hands not to worry."

She looked at him, "I don't know who you're speaking of."

He walks past her and whispers in her ear, "the cowhand who can't believe how pretty you are is helping the new men settle in." He walks on and into the judge's study and closes the door and Liss goes back to the kitchen.

The judge looks up and smiles, "how are the men Cully brought with him working out?"

"I can tell you they are good workers, don't have to be told more than once on a job and I tell you they got that fence back up and you'd never know it was cut."

"They're that good?"

"Like I said Judge they are good workers and we can start the branding tomorrow."

Eli smiled, "then it's settled, they're hired."

Jason smiles, "I'll go back to the bunkhouse and tell them the good news."

As Jason leaves, Liz looks at her daughter, Liss, get the table set or supper and tell your pa supper's ready."

"Yes Mama."

With that Liss knocks on Eli's study, "supper's ready Pa." She then makes her way toward the dining room.

The following morning, Jason and the men are mounted and ride out. It was just after sun up and as Liss looked out the window, she watched them ride off. The boys make their way to the north range and get ready to start the day when Jason noticed to the far end, smoke. It was in the direction of the Miller place and from the looks of the smoke, it wasn't a brush fire.

Jason looks at Cully, "what you make of that?" He points to the smoke.

"It doesn't look good. Maybe we should ride over?"

"I'll have the men set up for branding, then you and me head over to the Miller place."

"Think they're in trouble?"

"Well. the family moved out a few months back. Mr. Miller wanted to have his family safe at the fort in case the Sioux started up."

"Sioux? Has there been any raids, I mean…"

"Nothing so far, unless what we find up there changes it."

They head up the trail. What they found was the ruins of what the Miller family called home. The house and barn were just chard wood with flames sending its black smoke climbing to the sky.

Jason looks at Cully, "I'm glad Miller took his family to the fort. I mean look at this place!"

Cully gets off his horse and looks at the remains of the house. The devastation was like what he saw at the Cummings ranch, only this time it was different. He looks up at Jason, "this wasn't done by Sioux Jason. This was done by whites."

"Whites? "Are you sure?"

He hands him an arrow from the door of the house, "this not a Sioux arrow, this was not made by an Indian, but a white man." He walks over to the barn along the way he points to the hoof prints of the horses, "their

Indian ponies are not shod." He then points to the foot prints, "Sioux braves don't wear boots."

He looks at Cully, "how did you know?"

Cully just smiled. "when you've been around a lot, you learn the signs, and I had a good teacher."

"Would you have any idea who would want to do this?"

"No, but someone is trying to start an Indian war."

Suddenly, Jason looks up on the hill where two braves are looking down at them. Jason reaches for his gun, but Cully stops him, "They're not after us."

"How do you know?"

"If they were, we'd be dead by now."

Cully gets on his horse; Jason looks at him, "are we leaving?"

"Jason my friend, I'm gonna give you a rare privilege. You're gonna meet those braves."

He stopped for moment, "gonna meet… Ah Cully, maybe it be a better idea if I stayed back here. I mean you can meet them alone. I mean they may not be friendly with a person in uniform…You know I can sorta stay in the rear…"

Cully moves closer and hits the rump of Jason's horse and the horse takes off. As they draw closer to the two braves. Cully lifts his hand in friendship.

"I hope you speak their lingo."

"I do; not to worry Jason."

He looks at the braves, "I am called, Cully, great grandson of Evening Star, daughter of Black Hawk."

The taller of the two speaks, "I have heard of your grandfather. Many stories have been spoken, time and again about his bravery. I am is honored to meet his grandson. I am Brown Bear and this is my brother, Spotted Pony, our father is Night Wind, he is medicine man of our village."

Cully nods at the other brave. then again looks at Brown Bear, "May I ask what brings you two beaves so far from you lands?"

"We seek fresh meat for our village, since white men have come to our land, they killed many buffalo and took the hides and left the bodies to rot. Our people are starving. We hear the crying of the children in the village; they grow weaker each day, some have already died."

Cully looks down, he knows he has heard this story too many times, Buffalo hunters kill the herds and only take the hides. "I ask you Brown Bear, if I was to give you four cows to take back to your village, would that help the people and the children and make the little ones smile again?"

The brave smiled, almost in disbelief, a white man is offering to help them, "we are honored by your kindness and we will sing praises for you at our campfire."

"Jason, do you think we can spare four good sized cows for our friends here?"

Jason smiled, "I'm sure something can be arranged."

"Then if you both will join us, we'll see to getting you those four cows."

Brown Bear smiles at Cully, "you are truly the grandson of the great one, I will tell my father of your kindness."

Cully looks at him, "perhaps you may help us on a matter."

"Ask and if I can, I will."

"You saw the destruction down below, would there be anyone who would want this blamed on the Sioux?" He looks at Brown Bear

"There were raids near the fort, they, also, not Sioux, someone is trying to start a war." Brown Bear looks at him, "our chief passed on five moons ago; we still have no chief. Without a chief, we cannot attack."

Cully looks at Jason, then the brave, you need to keep your people on their land, I will tell the soldiers at the fort you did not do this. But I need your word you will not leave your village."

"I will tell our father, but he will want to hear it from you."

Cully looks at Jason, then back to Brown Bear, "tell your father, I will meet him at his village when the moon appears the second time. We will speak of what has happened and find an answer.'"

The braves are ready to get back to their village, as they slowly make their way back up the pass Jason looks at Cully, "do you believe him?"

Cully looks at him, "I have no reason not to. Don't forget if he wanted to, he could have killed us back there."

"What stopped him?"

"He wasn't a war party, he just needed food for his village."

Jason moved over to the fire and poured himself a cup of coffee. It was Carter who walked up to Cully, "t'was a kind thing you did for those Indians."

Cully looks at him. "I couldn't have those women and children starve. It just wouldn't be right, besides hey didn't set fire to that farm over there, it was whites who did it."

It was late afternoon, when Jason and the men were heading back to the Circle C.

Eli and Doc Woodward were sitting on the front porch enjoying a glass of brandy and watching the sun. A smile came across he old man's face when he saw Cully. ' "I see the young man Cully is back."

Eli nods, "yes he was a life saver, he took back with him eight of the miners from the fort who were looking for work, and I needed ranch hands."

Doc smiled, "he's a fine boy Eli, but I'm sure you know that already."

Eli agreed, "yes he does seem a likeable fellow."

It was Jason who made his way up the porch, while the others went into the bunk house.

"Afternoon Doc. Judge, can I speak with you in private for a moment?"

Eli looked at him and decided the conversation would be better continued in his study, "you'll excuse us for a moment Doc?"

"Yes, by all means, I'll just sit here and finish my brandy and watch the sun."

Once inside Eli's study, Jason explained the day's events, starting with the branding of the steers, the finding of the Miller farm destroyed, meeting the two Sioux braves and of course giving four steers to the braves to feed their village.

At the end of Jason's scenario, Eli looked at him, "you mean to tell me you and Cully found the Miller farm totally destroyed and Cully was sure it was done by whites."

"He did point out the foot prints and we do know Sioux don't wear cowboy boots and their ponies are not shod."

"True, but his riding up to meet those braves."

Jason looked at him, "he did explain his grandfather was Black Hawk…"

Before he could continue Eli cut in, "you mean to tell me he is the grandson of…"

Before he could continue, Jason stopped him, "yes, he is the grandson of the Sioux Chief and that is how he knows things we don't understand and that is why when he says the Miller farm was destroyed by white men, I believe him. Judge, we were side by side with those braves like it was an everyday thing."

Eli looked at him, "and he took it upon himself to give four of my steers to these braves?"

"Well, I did believe they were telling the truth. When you consider that they at any time could have killed us both and the hands were too far away to help us."

Suddenly there was a knock on the door and Eli answered, "who is it?"

"It's Cully Sir, I would l like a moment of your time please."

He looked at Jason, "open the door." Jason walks over to the door and opens it, letting both Cully and the doc inside before he closes it again.

Eli looks at them both men address the doc, "well Doc, I thought you were still outside enjoying your drink and the sunset."

The doc smiles, "I was until… well let's just say that with that window open and your voice several octave's higher than usual, I thought I might be of service here, hopefully, not in the medical capacity."

Eli looks at him, "now Doc, you know very well…"

"All I know is I was sitting on your porch and then the peaceful afternoon was, how should I say, interrupted by your constant outbursts of attacking your foreman, if his actions, which in my opinion were excellent."

He looks at Cully, "would you care to add anything to this?"

Cully looks at the judge, "well sir Judge, you really can't blame Jason. He had no idea of let's just say I don't usually go around telling folks my family tree. Mind you, I ain't ashamed of it. I just don't want to deal with folks thinking I'm gonna steal their cows or run off with their women folk…" he smiles, then looks back at the judge,' "like I said, the foot prints were made with boots and we all know Indian's don't wear boots, nor do their horses. No, whoever is doing this is doing it for one thing. To run the Sioux out of this territory and take the land for themselves."

li looks at him, "you feel sure on this don't you?"

"Let's just say I've come across this situation before."

"Here in Montana?"

"It's been tried all over, seems where ever there are Indians, someone's always ready to take their land from them."

Doc Witherspoon looks at him now, "you seem pretty sure of this."

"I am Doc.'"

While Eli's office was busy discussing the fact that white men dressing as Indians to drive the Indians off their land; in a deserted cabin about ten miles from the fort and totally hidden from site sit four men in the shadows of the fire. Carefully they talk about the killing of Jacob Schummer; that happened last week. The event was told to them by a wire that was sent to Private Jamieson at the fort. Jamieson was Schummer's go between here in the territory and with his contact being in the army, he knew what their future plans would be on the Indian raids.

The state department was in no way going to stop their plans for the contract with the railroad, but right now the word from back east was to stop the raids. Seems there is some official trip from some political big wigs who plan on visiting the site of the Big Horn in a few weeks. Seems our friends in Washington want to keep things down until they return back to DC.

In the shadows, a short man walks closer to the fire, yet his face was still in the shadows, "I don't like it. We're taking all the chances while those respectable men in their respectable positions are getting all the profits. Just where do we get some recognition? After all, we're the ones who are taking the chances. How long do you think they're gonna wonder why can't they seem to find these Indians. And whose idea was it to kill the Cummings family?"

"He saw us! He knew we were white men!"

The taller one moved toward the fire, "until we get the word all the riads are held off. I will wait for news from DC."

One of the men looks at him. "Hey how do you get wires fron DC and not questions asked?"'

The man smiles, "simple, I have a mother who sends me a wire twice a month on how things are back home."

"A mother?"

"Yes my dear mother, who happens to live in DC."

## Chapter 6

It was the start of a new day at the Circle C and as the men make their way out of the bunk house, Liss Crawford is standing on the porch of her house. She gives a smile and waves to Jason and Cully and they wave back.

"Would you like a suggestion my friend?"

Cully looks at him as he mounts his horse, "well, it's what that suggestion is."

Jason smiles, "go over and tell that pretty gal good morning."

Cully looks at him, "you want me to…"

"I want nothing, I just think it would be nice to say hi to that pretty young gal."

Cully looks at him and Jason smiles back, "go on, you can catch up to us."

Cully looks at Liss, then back to Jason, "go on.'"

Slowly Cully makes his way toward the porch as Jason and the men head down the trail to work.

Carter makes his way toward Jason and smiles, "somebody better talk to that boy. That's a fine looking lady and well…"

Jason smiles at him, "I know what you're saying, but you know these country boys have some wild notions and…"

Jason smiles, "I can imagine, only I don't think that country boy is ready for that girl. especially when she's got her mind set."

Carter smiles, "oh I guarantee ya everybody knows what she's got on her mind. Maybe somebody should tell poor Cully."

Cully makes his way slowly to the porch and smiles as he comes to a stop at the porch steps. "Morning Miss Liss. It sure is fine day."

Liss smiles at him, "yes it is. I take it you got to explain everything to my pa and it's all squared away?"

Cully looks at her, "if you mean am I still working here, I guess, so I'm riding out with the boys and…"

He sees her smile, "well it seems they all are riding out and you well you're…"

He turns and sees the crew is way ahead, then turns to her and smiles, "you know you have a way of making a fella forget a lot of things and that could lead one into trouble."

Liss steps closer to him and smiles, "you afraid of trouble Mr. Cully?"

He smiles at her, "not from a gal as pretty as you, but I'll tell ya about that another time." He smiles and takes her hands in his and gently kisses them, and turns his horse and heads out to catch up to the others.

As he rides off, Liss hears her mother calling her and she goes inside still holding her clasped hands and smiling. His words still echo in her mind.

Carter looks at Cully who catches up to the group, "are you staying with us or just passing through?"

Cully smiles, "Staying, come on, we've got work to do."

It was mid-afternoon when the drovers took a break from branding for lunch. It was Cully who found Carter near a shade tree enjoying a cup of coffee and a cool breeze that was a welcome from a hot morning's branding. Carter looks out across the stretch of mountains that lay to the side of him. Beautiful, majestic and peaceful were all he saw each time he looked at them. So captured by the sight, he didn't notice Cully walk over to him.

"Beautiful ain't they?"

"Beautiful indeed. You know even when I was in the hills mining for the gold, I would take a moment to step back and just enjoy this beauty. It's as if the good Lord sat down and painted these colors for us to enjoy. I can see why the Indians love it so much." He looks at Cully and smiles, "but then again I guess you know that already."

How well he did know these mountains. they were a place where he felt close to his grandmother and her people. There was a whole connection with the Great Spirit that was part of him. His grandmother had taught him to always be proud of his ancestors and that they all were children of the Great Spirit.

He often wondered if the whites and the Sioux could ever live peacefully in this land; it was then that Carter looked at him and misread his thoughts. "She's a pretty little gal. You do know she's kinda sweet on you?"

Cully shakes his head, "come on Carter…. Why she's…" His mind trails off as in his mind he sees her face smiling at him.

Carter smiles and nods, "why any man would be proud to have her as his gal. And you heed my words, when you least expect it, some young buck from another ranch is gonna sweet talk her out of your arms and into his."

"Now Carter, ain't no such thing, 'sides she's still a little gal."

Carter looks at him, "little gal, you sure you know what you're saying? You sure don't look at her like she's a little gal and she sure looks at you in a grown up gal way." Carter realizes the subject for now was closed, but it would come up again and again until that stubborn young man admitted it to himself.

They ride on a bit when Cully slows up a bit and looks at Carter, "ya know I've been a thinking. Let me ask you, if you was me, what would you do?"

Carter looked at him and smiled, "well, I'll tell ya, if I had a pretty young gal looking at me the way Miss Melissa looks at you, I'd get off my horse and take her in my arms and never let her go."

"I see you mean just take…"

Carter smiled, "yes take her in my arms and never et her go. Listen Cully, you got a gal who doesn't care who you are or where you've been. A body doesn't find that often, sometimes, not even in a lifetime. But this much I can be sure of, you and that gal are meant to be and don't go a trying to say it ain't so."

With that speech Carter gets up and heads for the chuckwagon to hand his plate and cup to cookie.

It was late afternoon when the hands and Jason came back to the ranch. With the help of Carter and his men they were way ahead wth the branding and would probably be finished by next week.

Cully had asked Jason if he could speak to the judge about keeping the miners on as hands until their problems with the folks in DC got taken care of. As Cully headed to the bunk-house with the drovers, Jason headed to the main house. As usual these past days, Liss sat on the porch watching the hands as they rode in. Jason dismounts and smiles at her, "lookin mighty pretty Liss."

She looks at him and smiles, "thanks."

He saw her attention was down by the stable, so he went in the house. She sat for a bit until she noticed the bunk-house door open and Cully, unhitching his horse and walking him to the stable.

It was then she got the idea to meet him in the stable. Why the idea was perfect no one would see her and she could be with him. Slowly, she made her way down to the stable. As she passed the bunk-house, she could hear the sound of laughter; the men were playing poker and from the sound seems ole' Shep was winning. She slowly opened the stable door and saw Cully at the far end of the stable brushing his horse.

If there was one thing one could say about Cully, was he took care of his horse after working all day.

She made her way slowly to him and he not knowing she was there, kept carrying on a conversation with the horse. As Liss got closer, she could hear him speaking to the animal. "So you tell me Scout, how would you talk to the judge's daughter?"

Liss had to control herself from laughing when she answered, "well I'd turn around and say hi."

Cully lowered his head and slowly turns around and looks at her. "Evening Miss Liss."

She looks at him, "is that all you have to say?" She walked over to the horse and petted him, "You were just asking Scout here how he would talk to me, only funny thing is, Scout can't talk yet he seems to have no trouble getting my attention."

The horse seems very content with Liss' petting him.

Cully looks at her, "goes to show you, the horse has good taste."

Liss moves closer to him, "and what about you Mr. Cully, are you as smart as your horse?"

"I'm not sure what you mean."

"Well do you think you'd be staying on when the branding is over?"

"Well tell ya the truth Ma'am, I ain't given that too much thought."

She gives him a shy half smile. "Well when do you think you'll give it some thought?"

He looked at her, "you see there's this gal and mind you, she's a right pretty little lady… before he could finish, she moves closer and puts her arms around his neck. He takes her arms in his and gently holds them and continues, "like I was saying, I never did it much thought, but you see, like I said she's a right pretty gal and up until a few minutes ago, I didn't think she had even known …"

She looks up at him, all he could think of was her eyes. Now anyone looking at her could see those eyes of hers were golden brown with a touch of green like the grass in early spring. They were mesmerizing and had this effect on Cully even he couldn't understand.

"You didn't think I would have ever known what Mr. Cully?"

He takes her in his arms and moves her closer to him, "Miss Crawford, I have had feelings for you from the first time I saw you on the side of the road after you were thrown from your horse."

He gently kisses her and she moves slowly back to catch her balance. He looks at her and smiles and she feels she's been played for a fool. Michael Culhane, how dare you treat me like some … like some."

She raises her fists in front of her face as if to punch him and he stops her, "now now, Mz. Crawford, this is not the way a proper young lady should act."

She looks at him, "I'll tear your hide for this. I swear Michael Culhane, you'll be sorry you ever…"

He looked at Scout, "fancy that Scout, and me a true gentleman was going to speak to her father for her hand in…"

She doesn't let him finish. "Speak to my papa; I'd rather be married to a mule, than hitch up to someone the like of you."

Cully smiles at her, "you may be saying no, but your eyes are screaming yes."

She picks up Scout's bridal and throws it at him. "You keep away from me and don't you ever come near the house ya hear me or I'll tell my papa what you tried to do to me."

"I did nothing to you!"

She smiled, "but my pa don't know that."

Suddenly there was a voice from across the stable and standing at the door was Eli Crawford.

"Mr. Callhan, I was told I'd find you out here tending to your horse. It seems there is the matter of the hired men we need to discuss, but I see I find you are in a bit of a problem here. Now I'm willing to hear your case, if you like." He smiles at Cully.

Liss looks at her father, "hear his case, but Papa, I'm your daughter, you should defend me!"

"Well you have to understand my point of view here, I came in the stable and see a young woman literally throw a horse's bridle at this young man, a young man who works for me."

Liss looks at her father, "but Papa, that was me! I threw the… oh you knew it was me."

He smiles at her, "aright, what did he do that got you on the war path?"

She looked at him and then to Eli, "he kissed me."

Eli looked at Cully who nods, then back to his daughter, "and you want him shot for that? Seems to me you'd like that."

He looks at Cully, "do you have any complaints about it?"

Cully looked at her, "No Sir."

Eli looked at them both, "then I think we can say it was a pleasurable experience for both of you. Now with that out of the way I would like to speak with Mr. Cully."

Liss looked at him, "I don't agree Papa, he told me he… oh never mind."

"Good then this is done. Mr. Cully, meet me in my study in ten minutes," he turns to leave, then turns to Liss, "and if my daughter tries to stop you, pick her up and carry into the house."

"Papa!"

Cully smiles, "I'll remember that."

Eli smiles, "you two decide that you more than just like each other, I'll be waiting for you in my study."

With that he heads out of the stable.

Cully looks at her and smiles, "so can we agree we like each other?"

Liss shakes her head no.

Cully looks at her, "what do you mean no? Liss ,I told you…"

She stops him before he can go on, "you told me many things, but I never did hear the word love in there."

Slowly, he takes her hand and draws her to him. He cups her chin with his left hand and gently places a kiss on her lips. He looks into her eyes and softly says, "Melissa Crawford, I have loved you from the first day I saw you on the trail. I wouldn't have come back if I didn't." He smiled at the look of shock on her face. "Well you got what you wanted, you got me to tell you I love you."

She put her arms around him and kissed him, "I love you too."

From the window of the judge's study, the voice of Eli can be heard, "if you two are done, I'd like to speak to Mr. Cully."

They both smile and hand and hand head out of the stable and toward the house.

The following morning, a young brave makes his way toward the Circle C; it was Brown Bear and he was hurt pretty badly with three bullets in his back.

It was Jason who noticed him by the corral and called for help. Carter and Cully came rushing out and one of the others ran up to the main house to get the judge.

Gently, Cully took him down from the saddle, the brave looks at him, "I came to find you Cully. I know where the white men are hiding." Cully looked at him, "let me get you some help," He looked up at Jason, "he needs a doctor Jason.'"

Jason looks at one of the men, "Ride off and get Doc Whitherspoon, tell him we need him now."

The drover heads to his horse and rides off.

The judge makes his way to the bunk house, he sees Cully and Brown Bear as a few of the gang help the brave up and take him to the bunk-house. He stops Jason as they all head back inside, "I take it that's the young buck, Brown Bear, you two met a few months back near the Miller farm."

"Yes sir it is."

"Did he say who shot him?"

"No sir."

"We'll see what Cully can get out of him, did you send for the doc?"

"Yes sir Doc Witherspoon."

"Fine, keep me posted and let's keep this just among the Circle C folks 'till we know what is going on."

It was mid-morning when Doc and the ranch hand arrived at the Circle C. As he stopped at the main house, he saw Eli sitting on the porch and smiles at him, "I was told to come here; someone needs my attention."

Eli looks at him, "you just take good care of the boy down in the bunk-house Doc, we'll talk later."

The man nods and heads down to the bunk-house. The doc gets out of his carriage and is met at the door by Jason. "Hey Doc."

"Jason, I heard you got a patient in there for me to look at."

"Sure do Doc, and let me say you got your work cut out for you."

"I see."

"Doc, it's Brown Bear."

Doc looks at him, "I'd better do a good job."

They both walk into the bunk-house. He sees Cully and nods, then leans down and looks at the boy's wounds. "Well Brown Bear, seems you got yourself in a bit of a mess. How did this happen?"

It was Cully who began to speak, "you see Doc."

Doc smiles at him, "Mr. Cully, you have a way of always turning up when folks need my services."

He looks at the man, "seem that way Sir."

"Well go on,"

Cully looks at him as he opens his bag and begins attending to Brown Bear. "Well, the story Brown Bear gave me was he was with the other braves out hunting on their side of the mountain. You do know that there's hardly any Buffalo left now that the hunters have killed off most if the herds."

Still attending Brown Bear, the doctor nodded and Cully continued. "Brown Bear told me he came upon these soldiers near the deserted gold mines."

The doc looks at him, "soldiers?"

"That's what he said, he said they spotted him and started shooting, as you see they got him in the back.'"

The sound of one if the bullets falling into the pan beside the bed told Cully that the good doctor was not only listening to him, but was doing his job.

The doctor looked up at Cully, "go on with your story? Why were they at the old mines, I thought it was Indian land?"

Cully looks at him, "that's what's got me a thinking Doc, something is not right."

The sound of the last bullet in the pan put a smile on Doc's face. "I've done all I can do, he's gonna need rest for a few days. Is there anyway word can get to his village?"

Jason looked at Cully, the doc looked at him, "do you think you could find the village?"

Cully looks at them both, "it shouldn't be too hard to find, but what do you expect me to tell his pa when he finds his son was shot by soldiers on their own land? You don't know his pa is."

The doc looks at him, "not unless you tell me?"

"His pa is Night Wind."

Doc looked at him, "you mean this is …"

Before he could finish, Cully answers, "seems those solider boys thought they were just shooting and Indian; they had no idea they could start a whole war all over again."

"Why is you seem to just walk into these messes. By the way, how is that darling wife of yours. Is she around, I'd love to say hi to her."

Jason looks at Cully, "wife?"

Cully looks at them both, "yes, well I…"

"Yes Cully, how is that wife of yours?"

There's a knock on the door and Liss is standing there, she smiles and walks in, "Well Doc Witherspoon, it's so good to see you."

She walks over to Cully and puts her arms around his waist and gives him a hug.

Doc smiles, "I was just asking your husband where you were. I must have missed you when I stopped by the house earlier."

She smiled, "Papa told me you were down here and I couldn't not stop and tell you hello and insist you stay for supper."

"Well that's very kind of you, but I must get back to my place. Maybe another time."

"Oh I do hope so Doc." She smiles and shakes his hand and walks back up to the main house.

Jason turns to them, "did I miss something somewhere?"

The doc smiles, "I'm sorry Jason, but the first time I had met Mr. Cully, he had come to my cabin to shelter from the rain and young Miss Liss had had a bad fall from her horse. I had assumed they were newlyweds and they kept the game up. So I couldn't wait to play the game on them now." He looked at Cully, "unless you two did tie the knot since I last spoke with you."

Cully, "no, no, still single Doc."

The doc looks at him and smiles, "a shame, you both look so well together."

## Chapter 7

It had been over two hours since the good doctor had gone into the bunk-house and treated the young brave. Now it was the game of wait and pray, the boy seemed to be responding well to the medicine and with a little luck and as Doc said, "the good Lord willing, he'll be able to ride out in a few days." He looked at Cully, "so have you thought more of going to his father? A word of advice, my boy, do bring something they can use."

He looks at the doc. "last time we met, I gave them four cows. You can't expect me to give them the herd, can you?"

"I don't expect you to know, but these people are starving. These people are too proud to beg, but at this point, we have taken everything from them and still want more. You wouldn't be here today if those Indians didn't come upon him almost frozen that winter. And don't you be forgetting they're part of your heritage too."

Cully looks at him, he knew the old man was right. It was at this time Eli was getting a bit itchy waiting on the porch and made his way down to the bunk house. He knocked on the door and Jason let him in. It was Doc who greeted him, "well Eli, I was wondering when you would come on down."

The judge looks at him, then the boy, "well Doc, what's the prognosis?"

"Well, it's my educated opinion that after a few days of bedrest and care, this young buck can safely return to his village."

The judge looked at him, "and how do we tell his people about this?"

The doc walked over to Cully and put his arm around his shoulder, "seems our very own Cully has offered to do that honor."

Cully looks at the doc who just smiles at him.

The judge seemed interested on how this young man was going to just ride into the Sioux village. "Yes, I would be interested on how you plan on attempting this feat?"

It was Jason who came to the rescue this time, "well you see Judge, the two braves Cully gave the cows to last month, they seemed to have heard of Cully's great grandfather and the three of them formed a kinship…"

What does Cully's great grandfather have to do with this?"

Jason tries once again, "Cully's grandmother was the daughter of Chief Black Hawk."

Eli looks at him. "You mean to tell…"

Before he can finish, Jason nods his head yes.

"He's…"

Again Jason nods.

"So you're telling me Cully's a Sioux?"

"Well, his grandmother was Black Hawk's daughter."

"I see. So you're telling me that Cully can ride into this Sioux camp and tell them that one of their braves was shot by the soldiers and they're just gonna let him ride back out."

The good doctor tries to explain, "Eli, you do know this chief Jason is talking about is a powerful warrior and is respected by the Sioux as well as other nations."

Eli looks at him, "you really think they will let him ride out of the camp in one piece?"

The doc smiles, "they might even make him a chief."

Cully looks at the judge, "Sir, there comes a time in one's life you have to take that chance. Now we gave those cows to that village; that has to be something in our favor. They also know we know they didn't do those raids, I figure with those odds, I've got a good chance of coming back."

Suddenly, there's a voice form the doorway, "mind if'in I add my idea on this matter?" Carter moves inside the bunk-house. "seems to me, you fellas are in a bind.

Now you need a way to get up in those hills without either side seeing ya." He smiles, "that's where I come in. You remember I know every rock and twig up there and there are three mines that still have not been touched. As I figure these soldiers boys are hiding their outfits in one of these mines which is how they can raid and turn into soldiers so easily that they're not caught."

Eli looks at the man, "you know, it just might work. Sending the two of you up there and maybe finding their hideout and bring down…"

Suddenly, there was another figure at the door, "In case you men didn't realize these folks you're talking 'bout don't care who you are if you're going up into the hills, you're breaking the treaty and…"

Cully looks at Liss standing there, "no one is breaking any treaty and…"

You seemed to forget all you and Carter have to do is go there and both sides have a reason to start a war!"

Cully slowly takes her arm and walks out of the bunk-house with her.

Eli shakes his heads and looks at the others, "I wish him luck at changing her mind."

Jason looks at him, "he'll need a miracle, not just luck."

The men watch as Cully gently but firmly escorts Liss form the bunk-house and into the barn. Once inside, he lets go of her arm.

As she stands there with her arms crossed, he looks at her, "I know what you're gonna say, but you have to believe this is the only way that there would be no blood shed."

"No blood shed! How can you say that! You do realize that in the bunk-house over there is one of their braves and he was shot, do you think you can just walk into their village and…"

He looks at her rant and carrying on and smiles. As she continues, he just looks at her and smiles wondering how in the world she could carry on and still look beautiful.

She looks at him, "Mr. Cully, are you listening to me?"

He moves closer to her and takes her in his arms, "I'm listening to every word you're saying."

"You don't seem to be listening."

He gently places a kiss on her cheek, "how can you say that?"

She tries to push him away, but he just tightens his grip around her. "You know you really are beautiful when you're angry."

Mr. Cully…."

"My given name is Michael, my ma said she named me after the arch angel."

She looks at him, "is that how you figure yourself Mr. Cully?"

He looks into her eyes, "I don't see me as an angel Miss Liss. Angels never fall in love.'"

She smiles at him. "Oh and you have Mr. Cully?"

He puts her arms around his neck, "let's just say I have someone in mind, if she's interested." He lowers his head and kisses her.

Back at the bunk-house, when Eli and the boys didn't hear any voices from the barn, it was Jason who asked, "she's stopped yelling, do you think they're okay?"

Doc smiled, "my money's on Cully and if I know that boy, I'd be betting he's got her just where he wants her.'"

Carter laughs, "I'll agree with you on that, only our boy thinks he's on the winning side."

It was late afternoon when Carter and Cully set out for the mountains. As they rode off. Liss stood on the front porch watching Cully smile at her and ride out of sight.

Carter looked at him, his eyes forward never turning once but the look on his face told the man his mind and thoughts were on her.

Back at the fort, Jamison had gathered his group for a quick run-through of tomorrow's raid. There was to be no changes from the usual. Attack farm houses; leave the proof it was done by the Sioux and after that, head to the cave; change into their uniforms and report to the fort about the attack.

A young private asked a simple question why and was told to leave. Jamison then proceeded to inform the remaining group they are under orders from the government to raid these farms as Sioux to force the officials in Washington to send in reinforcements to remove these savages from the territory and the railroad can use the land to expand the borrowers by laying down track and having the railroad join the east and the west.

A young trooper raised his hand, "isn't that breaking the treaty?"

Jamison looks at the boy, "Trooper, they are the ones breaking the treaty, not us."

He looks around the room, "if there are no more questions, we leave tomorrow morning for routine patrol and we return when we are done. That is all."

Chapter 8

Cully and Carter reached Brown Bear's village and was greeted by Spotted Pony, "Cully I am pleased to greet you here in my village, we are in sorrow at the loss of my brother."

Cully looked at him, "your brother is not dead. He is at the Circle C, recovering from his wounds."

The boy's face lit up, "this is true? Brown Bear lives?"

Cully nods, "it is true."

The by smiles, "Come, we must tell my father; he will be pleased."

Cully and Carter follow the boy to the teepee on the right of the camp. The young boy enters and in a few minutes, he emerges with an older man who walks up to Cully with a smile. "My son has told me of this good news. You are the one who is responsible for the smiles on the children's faces I am told. I, also, am to thank you for as my son now tells me about you saving my son's life. I am grateful and humbled by your kindness. I am Night Wolf Medicine Man of this village."

Cully looks at him, "Night Wolf, I am here not only to bring you the news of your son. I have come to ask a few questions on what's been going on and your people have been blamed for.'"

Night Wolf nods, "we will speak in my teepee." He enters his teepee followed by Cully, Carter and Spotted Pony. Once seated inside, Night Wolf begins, "my sons told me you are the great grandson of Black Hawk. A great warrior. He is spoken of in campfires for his bravery."

"Yes I suppose he is; my grandmother told me stories of him; I never met the man but was told of his life."

Nighty Wolf looks at him, "I suppose it is hard to live in both worlds. Never knowing which one is right."

Cully looked at him, "Night Wolf, I would like to speak with you on this matter of your people being blamed for the recent raids on the farms in the area."

"Raids? I can tell you my braves have been on this side of the mountain. You have been kind to give my village fresh meat; the older ones and children once again have smiles on their face. How can we dishonor you and raid the farms of your people?"

Cully looks at him, "I want to ask you if you have seen anyone on this side of the range?"

Spotted Pony looks at him, "It was soldiers, they came our land, near the trail where the yellow stones are. They attacked us and left up the trial where the gold stones are."

Carter looks at Cully, "the gold mines!"

Cully looks at Spotted Pony, was anyone else hurt besides Brown Bear?"

"You did not see?"

"Brown Bear made it to the ranch badly wounded. We had no idea what had happened, but decided to try and find you to tell you he was with us." He looks at Night Wolf, "you have my promise I will find out who did this to your son and they will pay."

"By your law or ours?"

"Let's find them first, then we will talk.'"

Night Wolf looks at Cully, "do you know why your soldiers would do this?"

Cully looks at him, he knew the reason, but for now he had to keep it to himself. "I will go to the fort Night Wolf and when I speak with the commander there, I may have the answers for both of us." He gets up and the others follow him out of the teepee. "Night Wolf, I promise as soon as Brown Ber is stronger, I will bring him to you."

The man smiles, "you are truly a friend of my people and you honor your great grandfather. Until we meet again, may the Spirits watch over you."

They said their goodbyes to the people and slowly made their way to the trail leading to the fort.

It was Cully who slowed down and looked over to Carter, "tell me are you getting this strange feeling that these raids are somehow connected to someone at the fort?"

Carter smiles, "I was waiting for you Yankee boy to be able to see the light. I had been thinking all this time the raids happened after we left the hills. They be no reason for them braves to be raiding if no one was on their land."

Cully adds, "when the Miller place was raided, the tracks were men wearing boots and as you saw today, braves don't wear boots and their horses are not shod. So it would have to be men who can ride in the open without causing attention and have someplace to change and raid as braves."

They look to the right to the trail that would take them to the hills where the miners were.

Carter looks at him, "I'm game if you are to go into the hills and see if we can catch the fellas."

Cully smiles and heads to the bend and up the trail. As they near the first mine, Carter notices the pony tracks leading to the first mines opening. As they dismount, both men notice the hoof prints of the ponies are pones with shoes, they also see several foot prints also with shoes. Slowly, they made their way to the mine's opening and paused a moment before they entered.

Carter found the lantern and lit the wick as they made their way in. Across the empty cart used to carry the gold out were several leather fringed shirts with beads sewn in the leather. The pants were of leather to match the shirts and in the cart was an assortment of bows and arrows. Carter looked at Cully, "I think we found our war party. I also feel you were right all along they're white."

Cully takes a piece of one of the shirts and heads out. "I'm willing to bet, most of what was stolen from the ranchers are stored here in these mines and I want to know who they are."

"Where do we start?"

Cully gets on his horse, "I have an idea and it's gonna need some help from our old friend, Doug Stiles."

Carter looks at him, "are you talking about the same fella that was glad to see us leave?"

Cully smiles at him, "oh you don't understand, why Captain Stiles is real friend of ours; he just doesn't like to show emotions. It's not very military and all."

Carter shakes his head, but is still not convinced on what Cully is saying."

Back at the fort, Private Jamieson was in Captain Stiles' office trying to explain or convince the captain; he and five others were up on the northern end of the fort when they were attacked by a band of Sioux.

Upon finishing the report he looks up at the private, "I see as you have written here, Privates Cameron, Harris, Wilson Tryon and yourself were assigned to get the firewood on the north slope. As you were following your orders, you looked up and saw a considerable number of Sioux watching you."

"Yes sir."

"You also state, they at that moment came down on you and the others."

"Yes sir, they were circling the wagon with that yelling and..."

Doug stopped him for a moment. "Now let me understand what you saw? You saw a band of Indians heading in the direction of all of you and of course you ran for cover."

Jamison nodded, "yes sir."

"Now you further state that in this battle, the Indians managed to ride off and you didn't see which way they rode."

Jamison looked at him, "Sir?"

"Well come now Private, we all are taught back in boot camp not only to defend ourselves, but if given the chance; see the direction the enemy is riding to."

Jamison looks at him, "well sir, we were trying to..."

Doug looked at him, "you're dismissed."

"Yes sir." He makes his way out of the office.

Back at the Circle C, Doc Witherspoon is tending to Brown Bear's wounds, being so busy he hadn't noticed Liss walk in.

She was holding in her hands a covered bowl of soup for the boy

Doc hears a creak in the floor board and looks up at Liss, "well, have you come to help me nurse this young man or just to bring us some food?"

She smiled at the man.

Doc had an easy way about him and made one feel comfortable around him. That's what she liked about him when they first met those few months ago. Why it's hard to believe she hadn't known him all her life. She looked at the young boy then at Doc, "how's he doing Doc?"

"Well, I tell ya Miss, he's young and strong and that young fella Cully; he's gonna find out the truth to this; I stake my word on it."

She smiles when he mentions Cully's name, a smile comes on the Doc's face, "If I'm not mistaken, you kinda have a high opinion of Mr. Cully also."

She smiles again, "he always seems to be around and he is very sweet."

Doc looks at her, "you know I said it the first time I saw you two and I still feel it you two are destined somehow to be together."

She smiles at him, "maybe one day Doc, maybe one day." Liss leaves the bunk-house and makes her way to the main house where she sees her pa on the porch.

Eli sees his daughter heading his way, "afternoon Lisa."

"Hello Papa."

"How's our young brave doing?"

"Doc says he's coming along."

"Good."

She looked at her father, "Papa do you think Cully s right about the raids being done by our folks?"

"Well I'll tell ya something Liss, this feud betwicks the Indians and the whites has been going on for a long time and will be going on even after our bones are set in this dirt, but one day, someone is gonna show we can get along."

She looks at Eli, "And you think Cully…"

"I'm only saying someday this will all work out and maybe that Mr. Cully…of who you think highly will be the one to start the process."

Eli smiles as Liss gets up and heads in the house; it's obvious that little Liss has finally reached the stage of reckoning the joys and wonders of her first love, Not saying he's not liking the boy; he finds Michael Culhane charming, thoughtful, intelligent and most important; he sees the boy is totally captivated by his Melissa.

It was later that afternoon when Cully and Carter rode in the gates of Fort Bennett.

Cully looks at Carter, "seems it's gotten more folks since we left a few days ago."

suddenly Cully hears his name being shouted across the compound, "Captain Cully, Captain Cully…"

"He looked up and saw young Corporal Reynolds running to greet them. There was just something about that boy you could t help but like, "Captain Cully, I'm sure glad to see you.", He looked at Carter also, "good to see you Mr. Carter also."

They dismounted and Cully smiles at him, "is the captain in his office?"

"Yes sir, Captain Cully."

Cully looks at him and he once again answered "yes Cully." Cully opens the door and all three walk in and they find Captain Stiles pouring himself a cup of coffee, "look what the cat dragged in."

Cully smiles at him, "good to see you too Doug."

"So do tell me, you just passing through or leaving for the east coast or..."

Cully follows him into his office, "you know from the way you're talking, one would feel you're not happy to see us, now I know that can't be. after all we were at the point together."

Cully looks at him, "I would love to go down memory lane with you Doug, but Carter and I followed a hunch and…" he takes from the inside packet of his vest and tosses the scrap of leather he took from the mine."

Doug looks at it and smiles, "it's nice, but really too flashy for me."

"We found it with others in the first abandoned mine in the hills."

Doug looks at him, "And?"

"And this is where they hide out or change! There are arrows shirts like this, Doug, it's why we are never able to find them; they have a hide out in the hills."

Doug looked at him and Cully noticed he had something hit him. Something that could maybe, just maybe be a real lead.

"Before you say anything. hear me out. There was a raid on our service wagon a few days ago. Private Jameson and four men were in the north ridge gathering wood for the fort as well as the families here. He and his men were attacked by a small band of Sioux. No one was injured and when I questioned if he saw the direction they were heading when they left, he said he couldn't tell. Now I found that rather strange and Jamison s not just a new recruit sent out here. Well, as I was saying, he said he had no idea which way they took off toward, but you know yourself if you're getting attacked from one side, you would think you'd… oh never mind.'" He takes the fabric in his hand, then throws it on his desk.

Cully could see frustration on his friend's face and that's something he could not have happen. "Doug, if these soldiers are the ones doing the raids dressed as Sioux, they have to be getting orders from somewhere and by who and why?"

Cully looked at Carter, "you said you got all your instructions from this Jacob Schumer; he was acting for the owners."

"That's right, his last wire to me told me the company was closing down and he would contact me when he found other work for us."

"So he had no idea himself who was also being closed down. Carter, you wouldn't have any of those wires he sent, would you?"

Carter looked at him, "no, I usually read them and tore them up like most people do."

Marty at this point smiles at them, "Mr. Cully, the telegrapher, he has copies of all the wires."

"Are you sure Marty?"

"Yes sir, I mean… I know this 'cause I saw him give a copy to Private Jamison one day."

Doug looked at Marty, "Private get the telegrams?"

"Yes sir Captain, he's got an aunt in Washington who sends him a telegram regular."

"She does seem like an awful nice lady."

Cully looked at the boy, "how do?"

"Sir?"

"You said she seemed like a nice lady and I said how so?"

"Oh at first she sent him a wire every two or three months, then it was every month."

Doug looked at him, "and what did she say in the wire?"

Marty looked at him. "Oh, I'm not allowed to read a wire Sir, you know the rules."

"I also know that he must have said something to someone. Who does he usually pass time either?"

Cully looks at Marty, "Marty, I wonder if you could go down to the telegraph office and ask the telegrapher if he just might have copies of the wires that were sent to /private Jamison."

"Copies Sir!"

"Yes, I know that they always keep copies of wires, it's a means of protection for them in cases like this when we want to find out who sends the wires."

"I'll be happy to go ask Mr. Cully." With that he's out the door and heading to the telegraph office.

Carter smiles at Cully, "you do know you made that boy's afternoon with that errand."

He looks at Carter as he continues. "we know Jamison gets a wire every week from DC from his dear sainted aunt and not too soon after that there's a raid, Now unless it's just a coincidence that after he gets a wire, there is a raid, then we have to assume it's a signal of some sort."

The other two agree on that thought as they wait patiently wait for Martin's return.

As the afternoon sun begins to makes its way in the sky toward the west a downhearted Liss makes her way in the house.

Liz sees the downhearted look on her daughter's face and tries to offer a word of encouragement. "You know he will be back."

She looks at her mother, "Mama, sometimes I wonder if he will or just keep going."

"Not that boy, I've seen the look in his eyes when he talks to you. If he had thoughts of leaving in the beginning, they are long gone now."

"Why didn't he come back after he was at the fort before."

"No my dear, that man has only one point his compass is pointing and that's right here." She smiles and heads upstairs to her room. Liz wishes there was something she could do to get that ole Liss back, but seems the only way that will happen is for Cully to walk through that front door.

She walks to the back of the house and to Eli's study. "Eli, I'd like to talk to you about something."

Eli looks up at her, "I would love to help you Liz, but at the present I seem..."

She slams the ledger book he has opened and looks him straight in the eye. "You will, make the time.'"

"Alright, what is the problem, Elizabeth?"

She looks at him in disbelief, "have you noticed our daughter at all?"

"Liz ,what is the problem, I'm very busy?"

"You do recall we have a young beautiful and very emotional young daughter who is feeling she is worthless right now because a certain young man still has not returned back"

"There's no reason for her to feel that Cully is not coming back; he assured me he would return."

She threw hands up in the air, "and how do you know that this my husband, how do you know that? Just because he told you he would return he would?"

He sat back in his chair and smiled at her, because I'll tell you, my dear wife, it's simply because a young lawyer spoke the same words to a senior partner of a law firm in a small town in Virginia. You see the young man, also had fallen in love with the man's only daughter and there was a little dispute, called the war, that he promised to serve and serve he did. Now, as I recall, those two had a rocky start, but I do believe things worked out well for them, don't you? By the way, did I ever tell you how much I love you?"

"Many times a day without even saying it." She starts to leave when he takes her hand. "Don't worry, they will find their path together."

She smiles at him, "I know," and then she leaves.

It was desk when four figures scurried from the back gate before walking their horses, so not to be noticed. Once Jamison and the men mounted their horses and headed in the direction of the hills, it was Marty that noticed the back gate was slightly open and went there to look at what was going on. Jamison turned and fired, hitting him in the shoulder and he rode off, not waiting to see if the young boy was dead or alive.

The sound of the shot was heard by the soldiers, but it was Cully who reached Marty first, "Marty, who did this to you?"

The boy looks at Cully, "it was Jamison. He and the others headed toward the hills. I'm sorry I couldn't stop him."

Cully smiles at the boy, "you did a good job, a real good job."

The boy smiled as three other troopers helped him into the doctor's office.

Cully looks at Doug, "well I guess we have our answer, don't we? I'll go bring them back for you."

Doug looks at him, "remember Cull, alive,"

He smiles at him. "if at all possible, Doug, you know that." He mounted up and they headed out. The troops did have a slight at advantage over Cully, they had no idea.

Carter had known all the shortcuts to the hills and they would be able to surprise them.

The troopers reached the mines, dismounted, and Jamison begin shouting out orders, "take everything out of the mine, we need to burn them. Take the gold and put it in my saddle bags."

For some reason, the men did not move. Again, Jamison fires orders; you all lost your mind. I said get the gold. Get it now."

The men continue to stand by their horses. Slowly, Jamison turns around; above him on the ledge were Cully and Carter and a few Sioux braves.

"It seems your men are not interested in obeying your orders Private and to their advantage, I would suggest they toss their guns down and surrender. Now you do how a choice Private, you can surrender which is the wise choice since that could possibly save your life or let my good friends here deal with you, after all, it was the son of their medicine man you shot. The choice is your of course."

Jamison looks at him, "you expect me to believe you and a handful if savages can take on the United States Army?"

Cully looked at him, "did I not tell you Private, look behind you as you can see if you gently turn around there are a few more of those savages as you call them."

He looks behind him and slowing tosses his gun to the ground, Slowly, the other troopers threw down their guns and Carter places them all in the nearby cart.

Cully looked at the troopers, "well I must say, it has been an interesting trip and I'm sure it will be just as interesting upon returning to the fort."

Jamison smiles at Cully, "do you really think that you and that old man are gonna be able to us four back to the fort?"

Cully smiles, that smile he always used when he knew he had the upper hand. "Tell ya what Private, I thought you'd kinda have concerns about this, so I've asked my good friends here to follow us at a safe distance until we reach site if the fort."

Jamison looks around and sees the hillside filled with Sioux braves. He looks at Cully who smiles at him, "just wanted to make sure you got back safely."

The sun was beginning to rise when Cully, Carter and the soldiers made their way to the front gates of the fort. Once they were recognized by the sentry, they were let in and Cully ordered the soldiers be sent to the brig. He then inquired about Corporal Reynolds and was pleased to know the boy was recovering from a wound to his shoulder. Both he and Carter then proceeded to go to Captain Stiles' quarters. They walk in to his office and find Doug sitting at his desk. "Well, I'm game to hear and see you are back Cully. Mr. Carter, I'm sure being with Mr. Cully has given you an exciting two days."

Carter smiles, "Oh I assure you, it has been."

Cully looks at Doug, "You know Doug, there's been something that has been bothering me."

"Bothering you? Well let's have it."

"Near as I can figure out these here raids started about the time Carter and his men went into the hills for the gold."

Doug looked at him, "now you can't suggest it was Carter and his men."

"No nothing like that, but, also, about the same time you were sent four new soldiers which you asked for,"

Doug looked at him, "well you have to admit with all the raids going on we needed more men."

Cully looked at him, "then there was the orders I got from Washington. To report here and you would fill me in on my duties."

Doug looks at him, "look, calling you out here was not the wisest move, but I needed someone I could trust! I needed someone the Sioux would believe! Good God Cully, do you know the wealth that's in those hills! Why, those dumb Indians have no idea the…"

Cully had heard enough as he heads toward the door and Doug speaks again, "don't be so noble Cully, there's enough gold there to make us both wealthy."

Cully opens the door and looks at the orderly, "please take the captain to the brig until further orders are given." He turns to Carter, "I believe it's time we get these folks back to their homes and a normal life."

Three weeks had passed and Captain Stiles, as well as the soldiers who acted on his orders of impersonating the Sioux and the murders of the Cummings' family would send them all to prison for a long time as well as a dishonorable discharge.

It was a fine sunny morning as Carter and Cully set out to leave the fort. With peace with the Sioux, the settlers were happily moving back to their homes and Nathanial Carter had been asked to lead the wagons back home.

Cully remined at the fort until the new captain arrived and was there when young Corporal Reynolds returned back to active duty and promoted to Sargent.

It was then that Cully decided to head back to the Circle C. Seems he had unfinished business back at the ranch and a young lady he had made a promise to. He was taught a gentleman never goes back on his promise, especially to a lady.

It was a journey for him that seemed a lifetime. After years of being alone he had found that one true soul he wanted to spend his lifetime on this earth with. It was early dusk and after three days of endless riding, he began to see the outline of the main house, was just in sight. A solitary figure was sitting in the porch and when she looked up and saw the rider approach she knew. As he approached closer, she ran from the porch to meet him.

He jumped off the horse and raced to catch her in his arms. "oh Cully, you cane back!"

He picked her up in his arms and looked into her eyes, "I promised you I'd come back. I had to, I love you Melissa and always will!"

Many find the magic of gold on the hills of Montana Michael Patrick Culhane was touched the magic in the heart of one girl named Melissa

## THE END

www.ingramcontent.com/pod-product-compliance
Lightning Source LLC
Chambersburg PA
CBHW072237150726
48002CB00005B/2134